SECRETS AT SUNSET

JULIETTE CROSS

Cover Design by Qamber Designs

Photo Image Credit: Regina Wamba

Prologue

❧

~REED~

Sitting on the coffee table, Jonah's phone lit up and buzzed with a text for the third time that night. Probably one of his many girlfriends doing a booty call. He was into his second hour losing at beer pong, so I doubted he'd be much use to any of them tonight.

I frowned when his phone vibrated again with an incoming call. Weird. It was after midnight on a Friday. That couldn't be good. The second I picked up his phone and saw the name, my heart plunged into my stomach.

Anna was calling.

Immediately, I punched in Jonah's code and answered, walking out onto our patio away from the blaring music and the guys laughing.

"Anna, what's wrong?"

Because there was definitely something wrong for his fifteen-year-old sister to be calling at nearly one a.m.

"Jonah?" Her voice wobbled with tension.

I slammed the sliding patio door closed because I couldn't hear. But it wasn't the drunken backdrop of our apartment that was drowning her out. It was a similar noise coming from her end.

"Anna, it's Reed. Where are you?"

Because she sure as fuck shouldn't be at a party. Jonah's parents kept a strict curfew on their only daughter.

"Reed?" She heaved a shaky sigh. "I need Jonah to come get me," she whispered, fear in her voice.

I didn't even have to glance through the patio door to know Jonah wasn't driving anywhere.

"Give me your address."

"Um…" She sucked in a quick breath like she was trying not to cry. "I don't know."

Goddamn it.

I had already moved back inside, grabbed my keys, and was out the door before I asked, "You're in Beauville?"

"Yeah. It's a house on a cul-de-sac across from City Park." She was moving, then it got quiet as though she'd closed herself in a room. "It's Hyacinth or Elm Street. One of those."

Jonah and I lived thirty minutes away from Beauville in Lafayette.

"Are you hurt?"

I started my truck and pulled out of the apartment

complex. She hesitated long enough to turn my hair gray at twenty-one.

"I came with my friend on the cheer team. I just... I didn't know it would be like this. I shouldn't have come."

No shit. Jonah would lose his goddamn mind if he knew his sweet baby sister was at an unchaperoned rager.

Anna was a shy, straight-A student who spent her free time practicing ballet and reading fantasy books. She was also a strikingly beautiful young girl with dark blond hair, huge brown eyes and the sweetest, loveliest smile.

When I helped Jonah and his dad put up a new fence in their yard this past summer, it hadn't escaped my notice that Anna—reading by the pool in a baby-pink bikini—was growing up fast. After I'd chastised myself for being a pervert, I'd told Jonah he'd better get a big stick to beat the boys off now that Anna was in high school.

"Don't worry," he'd said. "I'll kick the shit out of anyone who dares to try."

"Where's your friend now?" I asked Anna, pulling onto the highway, heading to Beauville. I didn't like the idea of her alone in some back bedroom with a bunch of drunk teenage boys wandering around.

"She's outside, talking to Blake and them."

I clenched my fingers tight around the steering wheel. "Blake Guidry?"

"Yeah." Her voice was soft and small.

Adam Guidry graduated with us three years ago. His only claim to fame was never getting caught selling weed all the way through high school. His little brother, Blake, would be a senior by now. "Asshole" ran in the Guidry family.

"Anna, listen to me. Go sit in a well-lit room in the house where there are lots of others around. I'll be there in fifteen, twenty minutes."

I knew exactly where Adam Guidry lived, and I was going to break every speed limit to get there.

"Okay," she said softly and hung up.

Then I flew like a bat out of hell down the highway.

~ANNA~

I WAS SO HAPPY TO MAKE NEW FRIENDS ON THE cheerleading team this year. Especially Ashley. She was the most popular girl in the ninth grade. So, of course, I was excited to sleep over at her house after the football game tonight.

"Get ready for some real fun," she'd said as we crawled out of her bedroom window at 11:30 p.m.

I'd been thrilled when she'd insisted on doing my makeup and dressing me up in her clothes. Having three older brothers and no sisters, I never had a sibling bond over makeup, fashion, and nail polish. Yet I'd always been a girly girl. I loved dancing and my pretty pink leotards and silky ballet shoes. My mom was wonderful, but the two things she hated most were shopping and makeup. We were total opposites. So to have the most popular girl in my grade offer to give me a glow-up makeover after the football game? I was super grateful.

"Girl, you are going to spin some heads tonight. Wait till the boys at the party get a hold of you."

Granted, I'd been stunned myself. Between the smoky eye shadow, the short skirt, and tight top that accentuated how big my boobs had gotten over the summer—late bloomer—I looked like a senior, not a freshman.

I should've known right then. The feeling of unease was a warning that tonight wasn't going to be as exciting as Ashley had promised. Not the type of excitement I liked anyway.

Of course, when we'd snuck out of her room, I thought we'd be going to a party with our classmates. I had a serious crush on this super sweet and super-hot guy in my art class. Liam LeBlanc was funny and so easy to talk to.

When we'd hopped in the car with Missy, a sophomore cheerleader, she'd said, "Y'all are going to love this. Blake throws the wildest parties."

The only Blake I knew was the senior who'd been checking me out the entire game from the front row of the bleachers. He hung with a rowdy group of boys who always seemed to be getting into trouble at school.

Just last week, one of his buddies, Dylan, was caught vandalizing the boys bathroom. He'd drawn a picture with a Sharpie on the back of the door of Miss Robicheaux. The drawing depicted her with giant breasts and exaggerated, bushy pubic hair. Her legs were spread wide. There was a speech bubble by her overbright smile that said, "Welcome to the jungle." And a rough map of the Amazon was drawn next to her.

The only reason Dylan was caught was because he posted it to like a hundred people on Snapchat, one was Miss Robicheaux's niece, who turned in the screenshot to the principal.

And now, here I was at a party where Dylan was shotgunning beer in the living room, spilling it all over the nice carpet.

Reed had told me to stay inside around other people, but everyone in here was getting so wasted and high, it made me uncomfortable. If I knew them, then I might be able to relax. But this wasn't my kind of crowd.

And Reed! God, how humiliating.

Reed Robicheaux, my oldest brother's best friend, who I'd been crushing on and trying to impress since I was seven when he'd picked me up after I fell off the trampoline.

This was super impressive.

Jonah would've yelled at me and lectured me to death, but having Reed pick me up here was going to be beyond mortifying.

"Hey, Anna! Come shotgun one. I'll teach you how."

Dylan grinned like the devil himself, holding up a can of Bud Light while his buddies chuckled around him. They all stared at me expectantly, nudging each other.

Heat flushed my neck and cheeks. "Um, no thanks." Then I beelined for the hallway.

"You scared her off, D," one of them said on a laugh.

"She'd be more scared if she saw what I have in my pants."

I hurried faster as they laughed louder. A senior basketball player and a girl I didn't know disappeared into a bedroom, their mouths and hands all over each other.

Screw this.

I hurried through the kitchen and out the back door. The music was louder out here. Post Malone pumped hard while everyone was hanging around the pool. As I rounded the corner out of the open garage, I heard Ashley squeal and then a splash. Sliding along the shadows, I walked quickly down the driveway.

"Anna," called a male voice behind me.

Midway down the drive, I stopped and turned, my pulse fluttering in my throat.

"Where you goin'? Ashley's over by the pool." Blake hooked a thumb over his shoulder as he drew closer.

"Yeah. Uh…"

I honestly didn't know what to say without sounding lame. I shifted from one foot to another.

Blake was tall with a muscular build, although he didn't play sports at school. Most girls found him hot. Objectively, I agreed. But there was something about his gaze that made me feel like a mouse watched by a hawk. Like at the game tonight. Like right now.

His fingers slid around my wrist. "Why don't you come on back and sit with me? We haven't had a chance to talk."

The devious tilt of his mouth sent a warning chill down my spine. He didn't want to just talk, and I knew it.

"No, thanks." I stepped back, but his hold on my wrist tightened. "I'm going to head out. I've got to be up early tomorrow."

He laughed, the dark sound speeding my pulse with a touch of fear. His black eyes glinted by the light of the streetlamp. "Where you gotta be, little Anna?" He tugged me closer, then his other hand gripped my hip.

"Please, don't." I planted my hands on his chest and pushed, but he didn't budge. "I need to go."

"No, you don't." His eyes were glazed from whatever he'd been drinking or smoking.

"Let me go, Blake."

"Nah, I don't think I'm gonna do that."

I smelled whiskey on his breath as he bent closer and sucked my neck. "Stop it!"

I grappled with his hands, trying to maneuver out of his hold, but he was fast and strong, even while drunk. He laughed harder. Terrifying me was amusing him.

Then his hand was on my ass, and he yanked me against his chest, whispering in my ear, "You're fine as fuck, Anna. Give me a kiss, and I'll let you go."

"No."

I knew he wanted more than a kiss, and I wasn't giving him anything.

"You're a little cock-tease, aren't you?"

I cried out when he bit my neck this time, his hands all over me. "Please—"

Suddenly, I was pushed sideways and fell onto the grass beside the drive. Blake was on the cement, a larger figure straddling him, punching him in the face.

Reed.

They grappled on the ground, the sound of a fist hitting flesh and Blake grunting before he bellowed a sound of frustration. While Reed continued to pound him, Blake fought back. He finally managed to twist out from under Reed and stumble to his feet. He swung and missed when Reed ducked.

Then Reed landed a hard punch to the gut. Blake bent forward and shuffled back a few steps, coughing then chuckling to himself.

They were both panting when Blake stood upright, swiping blood from his nose.

"Damn, Robicheaux," he sneered. "You like that tight baby pussy, too, huh?"

Reed moved so fast he was a dark blur, pounding a hard fist into Blake's face that sent him sprawling to the pavement.

"Fuck," gurgled Blake as he rolled to his stomach and spat out blood.

"Look at me, Guidry."

I shivered at the cold, savage sound of Reed's voice.

When Blake didn't move fast enough, Reed planted his boot on Blake's hip and shoved him onto his back.

"You better not be too drunk to hear this," grated Reed, "because my words need to sink into your stupid skull." He leaned over Blake, who flinched at the sudden movement. "If you ever lay a fucking finger on Anna again, I will end you."

Then he strode over to me where I was still sprawled in the grass, completely dumbfound. Reed helped me to my feet and kept a strong arm around my shoulders as he guided me to his truck in the middle of the road, still running with the driver's door open.

He walked me around to the passenger side and opened the door. I hurried to get in. By the time I was belted, he was tearing off down the road.

I didn't make a sound as tears slipped silently down my cheeks. Shame engulfed me—at dressing so skimpy, sneaking out, and going to the kind of party I never should've gone to, at what Blake did and said to me, at Reed having to fight him off. And finally at the thought of what might've happened if Reed hadn't been there.

"Are you okay?" His fists were tight on the steering wheel, his right knuckles bloody.

I still couldn't speak, but I nodded when he glanced at me.

"Did he hurt you?"

"I'm fine," I whispered as he pulled to a stop at a red light. Then he turned his attention fully on me and reached a hand toward my face. I flinched. He clenched his jaw then gently wrapped his fingers around my forearm and pulled my arm away.

I hadn't realized I had my palm covering my neck where Blake had bitten so hard it stung. He hadn't broken the skin, but it was sore to the touch. I'd never kissed a boy, much less make out and get hickeys or bite marks.

The red light contoured one side of Reed's sharp features, while the other side remained in shadow. I'd never seen Reed look menacing, but that was the only way to describe the cold fury on his face as he glared at the mark on my neck.

The light turned green. He closed his eyes tight as he straightened in his seat.

"Fuck," he muttered before driving on. "What the hell were you doing there, Anna?" he growled as he turned into my neighborhood.

"Please don't yell at me, Reed. I know it was stupid. Nothing you say is going to make me feel worse about it than I already do."

He glanced at me, but I kept my eyes forward as he drove slowly down my darkened street. A few houses down from mine, he pulled over, parked, and turned the headlights off.

My house was dark. I could sneak in and then tell Mom in the morning that I'd decided to come home late when they were already in bed. Not a lie. I'd just omit why. I was a homebody, so she wouldn't bat an eye. I rarely slept over at friends' houses anyway. After tonight, I'd be staying close to home for a while.

Reed rested both hands in his lap, looking straight ahead.

"Those aren't your clothes," he rumbled low.

Self-consciously, I pulled on the hem, which was ridiculously short when I was sitting. Reed knew me well enough that this wasn't mine.

"They're my new friend, Ashley's."

"Any friend who dresses you like that and leads you into a pack of wolves is not a good friend."

"I'm fifteen, Reed, not twelve," I protested, my temper spiking that he thought I was a child being led around like an idiot. Of course, I was also being defiant because he was right.

He snorted at that, turning his head toward the driver's side window. "You don't belong there, Anna. With those guys." Then he swiveled his gaze, the full force of his clear blue eyes on me.

Swallowing hard, I finally said, "I know."

His hard gaze softened. He reached over my lap, popped open the glove box, and pulled out a travel pack of tissues and held it out to me.

I took a minute to wipe my face, my makeup obviously running from the black smudges on the tissue.

He sighed, his next words softer. "I know you're growing up and you're finding your own way, but don't change who you are to fit what others think you should be." He turned back to me, eyes piercing but tender. "Take it slow. Find the friends who care about you, who will be there for you. Not the ones who are going to take you and leave you stranded in the hands of someone like Blake Guidry."

He said the last words with a dark rumble of anger.

I'd balled up the tissue in my lap. My breathing was finally calm and steady. He wasn't looking at me with anger or pity or disgust, but like he usually did with that quiet attentiveness that made me feel safe.

"Thank you for coming for me tonight," I whispered. "And thank you for being my friend." The kind who was there for me.

His gaze turned serious and sincere. "Always, Anna."

Chapter One

❧

~REED~

"I can't believe my whole family is against me."

My stomach clenched at the sound of her voice in the Hebert's kitchen as I walked through the living room. I paused on a shaky exhale, their voices carrying.

"We're not against you, sweetie. Don't be so dramatic," said Anna's mother, Ms. Dinah. "We just want you to get more experience first."

"Your mom's right. It's a big step, princess."

I hesitated before I rounded the corner into view, preparing myself for the sight of her. It always took me a minute to recover. Sure enough, that visceral reaction I had every time I laid eyes on Anna Hebert punched me hard again, a jarring sensation that made me dizzy.

"Sorry to interrupt." I held up my portable ice chest. "Jonah out back?"

"Hey, Reed. You're not interrupting," said Ms. Dinah.

Anna's big brown eyes skated away from me to the floor. She was leaning against the kitchen counter in a casual summer dress that loosely draped her tall, slender frame. It was still May, but in Louisiana, it was already hot as hell. Her long legs distracted me for a split second before I cleared my throat and forced my eyes not to wander.

"Hi, Anna."

"Hey." Her gaze was still on the floor, and I wanted it on me. But if I stared any longer, her dad would notice.

"Jonah on the patio?" I asked again.

"Yeah, he's on grill duty." Jim Hebert clapped me around the shoulders as we walked toward the back door. "Brought my favorite, didn't you?"

"Of course, Mr. Jimmy."

"That's my boy."

The Heberts had a nice covered patio affixed with ceiling fans on the east side of the house. In Louisiana, that was important. It meant that you could actually come outside and enjoy the outdoors for most of the day, even in summer.

Plus, they had a pool. Currently, no one was in it. And I prayed that Anna wouldn't dare. There was only so much willpower a man could be expected to have. Sitting among her parents and three brothers and pretending I wasn't staring while she flitted around in a bikini was akin to swimming in bloody, sharky waters and hoping you didn't get bitten.

"Reeeeed!" shouted Jonah's brother, Justin. He was the second in line behind Jonah, but the biggest of the brothers, built like a pro linebacker. "Please tell me you brought the Old Fashioned mix."

"Of course." I lifted the ice chest and headed to the outdoor kitchen and bar that I'd built with Jonah a few summers ago. It was a Father's Day present for Mr. Jimmy. "Jessie, you want one too?"

Jessie was the third Hebert son, a year older than Anna. She was the baby. Jessie's head popped up from his phone. "Nah. I'm good." He held up the bottled beer that had been sitting between his legs.

"Was wondering if you were coming or not," called Jonah from the grill, shirtless and in shorts but wearing his mom's apron adorned with a crawfish wearing a chef's hat. The words below read, *First you make a roux.* "What took you so long?"

This was the first time I'd see Anna since she graduated from college in Lafayette and moved back home, so I'd debated for an hour if I should make an excuse to ditch the Hebert barbeque today.

"Just had a little job to finish up."

"Hale working you on Sundays?" asked Mr. Jimmy, setting four rocks glasses next to me as I unpacked my latest concoction of Old Fashioned in several mason jars on the counter.

"Nothing big," I told him, hating to lie, but I sure as hell wasn't telling him the truth.

"That doesn't look like your regular Old Fashioned."

"This is a new one. Blackberry."

After pulling out the ingredients I'd stashed in my cooler, I used a muddler to crush the fresh blackberries at the bottom of each glass. Then I filled each with ice and poured the mixture of aromatic bitters, rye whiskey, blackberry liqueur, and simple syrup. Finally, I rimmed each glass with a slice of orange and handed one to Mr. Jimmy.

"See if you don't like it."

The man who'd been like a father to me since I was in elementary school took a sip, his gray eyes lighting up. "Mmm. Son, you should get a weekend job as a bartender."

I laughed. "I prefer it as a hobby."

Mr. Jimmy carried three glasses in his big hands, walking across the patio to the grill to hand one off to Jonah then one to Justin.

"Can I have one?" came that familiar, sweet, devastating voice behind me.

My body locked up, but I turned casually to find her leaning on the bar to my right, staring at the fourth drink in front of me.

"Here. You can have mine." I lifted it toward her. "I can make another."

The way she was leaning had pushed the slender strap

of her blue sundress to the edge of her shoulder. It was about to slip off. Of course, that conjured images of me undressing her. Something I should *not* be thinking of right now.

She wore no makeup, and her hair was tied back in a loose braid, wisps of blond hair framing her heart-shaped face. She was still the most beautiful woman I'd ever seen.

"Thanks, Reed." She stood straight, flicking the dress strap back into place and taking the glass, her slender fingers grazing mine.

"Welcome."

"Since when did you become a mixologist?" After she took a sip, she closed her eyes, a hum of pleasure climbing her throat. "That's really good."

Jerking my gaze away, I pulled down another glass from the cabinet and started making one for myself. "Just a hobby," I told her. "Something I do to relax at the end of the day. I like to experiment."

"I'm more of a wine girl, but this is pretty amazing," she said brightly, still standing next to me at the bar.

I pretended her nearness didn't affect me like I always had. Like she always did. Watching my best friend's sister grow into a vibrant, sexy, intelligent woman was torture from a distance. Up close, she was frying my circuits and my ability to act casual.

"So what's on the agenda now that you've graduated?" I asked her as we walked over to the circle of patio furniture.

"Why don't you ask my dad? Because he's got it all worked out."

"Aw, hell," mumbled Mr. Jimmy, taking a gulp of his Old Fashioned.

I took a seat in a cushioned chair next to Justin. Anna sat on the loveseat across from me next to her dad.

"Wrong question," mumbled Jessie, never looking up from his phone.

"Jim! Come help me put the leaf in the table," called Ms. Dinah from the patio door.

"Coming!" Mr. Jimmy escaped with his glass in hand, obviously glad to get out of the conversation.

But I wasn't ready to let it drop. I wanted to know what was happening with Anna. "So what's your dad's plan?"

She tucked both legs up on the loveseat and sat sideways then rested the drink I'd made her on her hip. I tried not to focus on the hem of her dress hitting her mid-thigh, revealing a great expanse of skin and long, tan legs.

"Dad wants me to go work for Broussard Appliances." She rolled her eyes and sipped her drink.

Mr. Broussard was an old friend of Mr. Jimmy and had several appliance stores in town.

"With a business degree? He wants you to work at a local appliance store?"

She scoffed. "That's what I said!"

"Don't get her started." Justin shook his head on a laugh. "Once she gets going, she won't ever stop."

"Shut your trap, Justin."

There was nothing wrong with working local, but I always pictured Anna to be the one to get her college degree, leave Beauville behind, and set her sights on a bigger business elsewhere. I'd also imagined she'd have married that college boyfriend in pre-med and have the perfect house and 2.5 kids. Again, elsewhere.

I leaned forward, elbows on my knees, my glass hanging in both hands. "Yeah, I figured you'd move to Baton Rouge, get your MBA or at least look for something bigger elsewhere."

She tilted her head a little, studying me. "No, it's not moving away from Beauville that I want." Her sincere expression snagged me hard, as if she was disappointed I even suggested she should desire a life outside our small town.

Sitting up, I cleared my throat and took a gulp of my drink. "What is it you want to do in Beauville then?"

"She wants to open her own dance studio," blurted Justin with a goofy grin.

She turned a death-glare on her brother. "Do you mind? I'd like to speak for myself, thank you." She made a frustrated sound. "This is what the problem is," she told me with narrowed eyes. "Everybody around here still treats me like I'm ten, playing Barbies."

"So dramatic," huffed Jonah, carrying a giant platter of barbequed chicken toward us. "Listen to Mom and Dad, Anna Banana."

I caught her cringe at the nickname before Jonah added, "You need to build some experience before throwing away a shit ton of money on your own business. Now, come on, let's eat."

Justin popped up and hustled after him. "Ain't gotta tell me twice."

Jessie didn't say a word as he stood and slid his phone into his pocket, following his brothers silently back into the house.

Anna didn't move, her stern gaze on the patio floor. There was a deep vee carved into her forehead as she apparently grieved the fact that her family wouldn't listen to her. So I did the only thing I could. I listened.

"What's stopping you?" I asked quietly.

Her gaze shot to me, amber eyes round in surprise. She moistened her lips and swung her legs around, planting her feet on the concrete.

"I can use the money I saved in college for the down payment to buy the building, but it needs serious renovations to become the dance studio I envision. I'd need Mom and Dad to co-sign a larger business loan to make it happen."

She wasn't about to cry, but her eyes were glossy with emotion. More frustration and anger than sadness.

"You're resourceful, Anna," I told her.

Her expression softened into amused disbelief. "So much faith in me, Reed?"

I'd known Anna most of my life. I'd watched her accomplish every goal she set out to gain, and then some. She had been a straight-A student all the way through high school and graduated as valedictorian. She won multiple dance and cheer competitions. She earned a full-paid scholarship on her high ACT scores alone, even lived in the Honors dorm—rent free—through college. And she'd still waited tables to save a nice nest-egg, according to Jonah.

She'd always been the brightest light in this family. It physically hurt to see her feeling anything but their full support.

Granted, I understood what her parents were talking about. Opening any business, especially in a small town, was a big risk. But then Anna wasn't the kind of woman to take a risk without intelligent calculation of the odds.

"Is this what you truly want?" I asked her.

The gleam of joy returned to her pretty face. "More than anything. And I found this fantastic building in the historic district on Main Street." She cupped her drink with both hands, the glass propped on one knee. "It's absolutely perfect, Reed."

"It's not me you need to convince."

She glanced over her shoulder and blew out a frustrated sigh. "Trust me, they won't listen. I've been working on them since January. They're not giving in."

I shook my head. "Not them." I pointed to her. "You."

She blinked. "What do you mean?"

"If this is truly what you want, then figure it out. You're a smart woman, Anna. I know you can."

The patio door popped open where Jonah stood, now wearing a shirt. "What the hell? My chicken's getting cold. Come on!"

I let Anna walk ahead to join the family at the table. While I felt her gaze on me as we settled into the two empty places at the table, I didn't look at her again. I'd tortured myself enough for one day.

It wasn't that I thought I wasn't good enough for Anna. Not really. I just wasn't the kind of guy she wanted. She'd always dated the academic, high-achieving, brainy kind of guy. I was the one who squeezed by with Cs, determined to never enter a classroom again after high school.

Having ADHD had made school a difficult place for me to be. But it wasn't even that. My interests always had lain in doing something with my hands, working outdoors and not in an office. As often as I'd let myself fixate on Anna, I'd always known she would be nothing more than a fantasy for me.

"Let's hear it," said Jonah. "Is my chicken amazing or what?"

"Mmph," grumbled Justin with a mouthful.

"Reed?" Jonah arched a brow at me.

"Amazing. Best barbeque chicken I've ever had."

"Damn straight, it is." Jonah pointed a drumstick at me from across the table. "Better than Door Dash again."

I ignored his usual heckling and dove into Ms. Dinah's mac-n-cheese.

"You need to learn how to feed yourself," said Jonah.

Justin set his iced tea down with a clunk. "Or just get a woman."

"Oh, that's nice and sexist," snapped Anna on my right.

"What?" Justin gestured innocence. Poor man.

Anna rolled her eyes. "Just get a woman to cook for him? Did you leave your brain in the 1950s? No wonder you don't have a girlfriend."

Justin huffed. "What I meant was that girls are better at cooking."

"Really? Have you seen the number of male chefs on the Food Network?" she snapped.

"I don't watch those shows."

"You're an idiot." Anna shook her head.

"Well, you're better at cooking than any of us, and you're a girl."

Jonah nudged Justin with his elbow. "Bro, let it go. You're digging yourself deeper."

"Agreed," she said, pointing her fork full of green beans at Justin. "Just because I'm a better cook than any of you doesn't mean I belong in the damn kitchen cooking for a man."

Mr. Jimmy laughed at the head of the table and kept eating. One thing I loved about Mr. Jimmy and Ms. Dinah is they always let their kids fight it out. And nine times out of ten, Anna won.

Justin huffed. "See what you got me into, Reed?"

I blinked at him. "I never said a damn word. I'm perfectly fine eating take-out and my Nana's shrimp etouffee once a month."

"How's your Nana doing?" asked Ms. Dinah, taking the opportunity to change the subject.

"She's doing just fine."

"Oh, that's so good to hear."

My nana had raised me after my mom got sick and passed away when I was in ninth grade. I never knew who my dad was. Mom had always said *he's not worth knowing* and *we're better off without him.* She got pregnant at sixteen when he was working at one of the sugar mills during harvest season. He left town when he found out she was pregnant and never looked back.

Mr. Jimmy had always been the father I never had. The father that meant something to me.

I felt Anna staring at me again. Unable to control myself, I slid my gaze her way. That was a mistake. Those pretty brown eyes speared me, stirring that raw need always lurking just beneath the surface whenever I was near her.

Most of the time, I could keep my desire in check and well-hidden. But the examining gaze she wore right now, like she was trying to discover what I was hiding, delving deeper and getting closer, wrenched something loose behind my sternum.

When she finally looked back down at her plate, her mouth tipped up in a secret smile, the one that made me crazy to know what she was thinking. Instead of asking, I focused on eating dinner and not obsessing over all the ways I wanted Anna Marie Hebert.

Chapter Two

~ANNA~

"CONGRATULATIONS! BEST OF LUCK TO YOU."

"Thank you so much." I shook Mr. Viator's hand and waltzed out of the title office, clutching my folder of ownership documents in one hand and keys in the other.

The tight ball of anxiety centered inside my chest squeezed just for a second before I turned left on Main Street and started walking. I glanced around, afraid Mom or Dad or one of my brothers would just happen to drive by right at that inopportune moment. But two and a half blocks later, I was standing in front of my new building, what would become my very own dance studio.

My dream.

I inserted the key in the lock and opened the door, stepping into the dusty former insurance office. It didn't look any different than the last three times I came to look around. Half-walls were erected into cubicles in a large rectangular room. Toward the back, there were two offices and a bathroom.

Assessing once more, I imagined what it would look like with the cubicles knocked down and cleared out, the carpeting replaced with hardwoods, one wall covered in mirrors from end-to-end, a ballet bar on the right wall, and one of the offices in the back converted into a dressing/locker room.

That tight ball loosened and unspooled, allowing my lungs to fill with a breath of hope. Laughter bubbled up and then out, filling the high-ceilinged room, echoing in the empty space.

"I did it."

Well, almost.

Mom and Dad said I needed a plan. And I had one. Time to put it into action.

After locking back up, I hurried back across the street to Belle Teche Plaza where I'd parked my car. The plaza was in the middle of town between Main Street and Bayou Teche that wound through Beauville.

By some miracle, I didn't run into anyone I knew. I was pretty sure if someone had asked what I was doing at that moment, I wouldn't be able to stop from spitting out, *I just blew my life savings on an old insurance office.*

While I didn't have the money yet to convert the office into a dance studio, what I did have was a plan. The hard part was to get *him* to agree to it.

Jumping into my Honda Civic, I drove toward Broken Arrow Highway and the small one-loop neighborhood that was one of the last before there was nothing but sugarcane fields. When I saw Reed's work truck in the driveway with Hale Building Co. on the side, my stomach did a double flip.

Parking behind his work truck, I exhaled a deep breath and gathered my courage before stepping out of the car. The garage door was open. He wasn't in there, but his motorcycle was, giving me a *frisson* of excitement, scattering goosebumps along my arms. Just the thought of him riding that bike made my knees weak.

Reed's house was a small Acadian-style cottage with obvious renovations. Since he'd moved in, he'd painted the house moss green with white shutters and rustic wooden posts added to the front porch since he'd moved in.

I'd only ever been to Reed's house in the company of Jonah, and that had been exactly three times. The first was the weekend he moved in here five years ago. Mom and I dropped off housewarming gifts, a set of kitchen towels with tiny blue crabs on the trim, a new set of rocks glasses, and a casserole. Two Thanksgivings ago, we picked up him and his Nana when his work truck was in the shop. And last Christmas Eve, I drove him home from our family's party because he'd had too much of Dad's Bourbon eggnog.

I still remember the way he'd looked at me before he got out of my car that last time. A little bleary-eyed with that sexy, tilted smile. He'd opened his mouth to say something, but then he'd quickly shut it and opened the car door with a quiet *Merry Christmas, Anna.*

Now, here I was at his house…alone. The mere idea of being alone with Reed Robicheaux sent a blast of butterflies in all directions.

I went to the front door and knocked. A minute went by, and so I knocked again. Nothing. When I tried the door, it was locked.

I knew he had a workshop on the backside of the house. Maybe he was working out there. I walked around the back and had stepped onto the second stepping-stone leading to his workshop when a deep voice stopped me.

"Anna?"

I spun on the step to find Reed sitting on his back porch with a rocks glass in his hand, scowling at me.

Of course. It was late afternoon, the orange glow of dusk settling on the backside of his house. I'd heard him tell Jonah often enough he liked to try his new drink concoctions for his afternoon cocktail when work was done. Jonah always teased him about his affinity for whiskey cocktails instead of just beer, but Reed never seemed to care what others said about him. He had this *knowing* of himself that always inspired me. Comforted me.

"Hi!" I squeaked, then cleared my throat and walked closer to the back porch to stand at the bottom of the steps.

"What are you doing here?" Reed's concerned and somewhat annoyed expression hadn't shifted.

"Um, well…" I took two steps up the porch then froze. "Can I talk to you a minute?" I gestured toward the porch swing to his right.

Still wearing an ornery frown, he dipped his square chin.

Taking a seat, I set my car keys down and gathered my wits, trying not to focus on the dark scruff of his afternoon shadow along his chiseled jawline, his piercing blue eyes, or the way he tracked me across his porch like a tiger in the underbrush.

"So," I said matter-of-factly, "I took your advice."

"Which advice is that?"

"I bought my studio." I sandwiched my hands between my knees to keep from fidgeting, but I couldn't stop my knees from bouncing.

"I thought you said you couldn't afford the loan without your parents' approval. Did they finally approve?"

"No." I let out a nervous laugh. "I used my savings to buy the building. For the down payment, I mean. I'll still need to start making monthly payments by mid-summer. I needed my parents to help with another loan to renovate the space. Which is why I'm here."

"I'm sorry." He angled his body toward me. "Why are you here exactly?"

"I have a proposition for you."

His brow raised slowly in question, and I'm fairly sure, interest. But he said nothing, so I barreled ahead.

"You told me to be resourceful, which was great advice. So here's my proposal. I will clean your house and cook meals for you daily if you help me with the renovation."

Reed didn't react. As a matter of fact, I wasn't sure if he was even breathing as he continued to stare at me dead-on in an awkward silence.

After realizing he might need some persuasion , I continued quickly, "I'll do your laundry, sweep, mop every single day. And I'll have dinner waiting for you when you get off work. You'll save some money on take-out, but it'll be even better home-cooked meals. You can just come home and relax after working all day."

"Except that I'll be working on your reno after work. And on weekends." He wasn't frowning, at least, but his mind was calculating the late hours.

"True. But also, I can help with demo, removing the cubicle walls in the space. And if you show me what to do, teach me, I'm a great student." I said the last on another nervous laugh.

His intense gaze swept briefly down my legs, and then he stood and leaned on the pillar of the porch, propping his tumbler on the railing. He swirled the glass, which was sweating from the afternoon heat. The ice tinkled.

"Your parents would kill me if they found out I was going against their wishes."

"No, they wouldn't. They love you like their own."

His shoulders stiffened. "Until they realize I went behind their backs."

After standing from the swing, I walked over and leaned my hip on the railing, facing him. "If you don't help me, I'll have to find someone else. I've bought the building. It's done. I have a bit of money left over for supplies but not the labor, and I need a professional." I glanced off into the yard. "Maybe Hale would help."

I bit my lip, wondering if the devilish Hale Broussard would exchange labor services. Or if he'd just use the excuse to try to get me to go out with him for the hundredth time.

"The hell you will," grumbled Reed, straightening to his full height. I always forgot how tall and broad he was until I was standing right in front of him. "You're not going to Hale."

The sun was sinking behind the trees of his house, gilding half of him in light, the other in shadow. I always felt like Reed was two different men. The one I saw and knew so well and the one he kept hidden from the world. What I wouldn't do to know all of his secrets, to know all of him.

"Then you'll help me?" I asked, hopefully.

His stormy gaze swept across my face, a pinched brow set deep in concentration. "Yes, Anna. I'll help you."

I burst into laughter and wrapped my arms around his neck, hugging him tight. How did a sweaty man smell so good?

His body stiffened, then slowly curled around me, one arm wrapping my waist.

"Thank you so much, Reed. This means the world

to me."

His arm tightened around my back before his hand found my waist and nudged me away. He averted his gaze to the yard as he took a step back. "Send me the address, and I'll meet you there tomorrow at five."

Clapping my hands together, I went back to the swing and scooped up my keys.

"Wait a minute," he said, carrying his glass back into the house and returning thirty seconds later with a key in his hand. "You'll need this to get in during the day."

When Reed put the silver house key in the palm of my hand, a buzz of awareness rippled through me. Now one of his secrets was mine as well. A mellow warmth seeped right into my bones.

I quickly slid the key onto my keyring and looked up to find him examining me closely. He often wore this expression when he looked at me, full of intense scrutiny and a deeper emotion akin to compassion. Or admiration?

Yes, he was my brother's best friend and he'd treated me like his little sister all my life, but that wasn't what I felt when he looked at me this way. And I definitely had zero sisterly feelings for him.

Seeming to catch himself, he cleared his throat and took a step back. "I'll see you tomorrow at five."

"Tomorrow," I agreed with a smile then turned and hopped down his porch steps.

As the last sliver of sunlight slipped behind the trees, I felt the thrilling weight of Reed's gaze hot and heavy on me as I walked away.

Chapter Three

❧

~REED~

To say I'd been distracted today was an understatement. I'd missed my Wednesday morning meeting with Hale and his other foreman Bernard. We always had a mid-week morning check-in on our jobs since we each led our own crews. But I'd totally spaced today.

Wonder why.

Hale didn't call me on it, but he did give me the side-eye when I was only half listening to him go over the inventory coming in for the residential job I was in charge of this month. I was unfocused, but there was no way to snap out of it. Not when I knew I'd be seeing her today.

Shoving my truck into park in the plaza right next to Anna's car, I then jogged across the street, pulse jackhammering hard. The front windows were still covered in blinds, the logo for Romero Brothers Insurance still embossed on the glass door. I pushed the door open to the sound of loud banging and Billie Eilish playing on blast. I smiled till I rounded the corner and saw her.

Sweaty and her threadbare pink T-shirt sticking to her torso, she was bended over and swinging a sledgehammer at a partition wall. Her short denim cut-offs rode so high I nearly choked on my tongue. I had to close my eyes and count to ten so my dick wouldn't be a giant bulge in my jeans by the time she noticed me.

Snap!

I lunged forward as the half-wall collapsed with Anna on top of it, unable to stop her momentum.

"You okay?" I plucked her up by the waist with one arm and took the sledgehammer from her with the other hand. I scowled at the fact she hadn't even been wearing gloves, which was dangerous for demo work

"Oh!" Her eyes widened as she looked over her shoulder and wrapped her fingers around my forearm, seeming to hold me there rather than push me away.

Realizing I had her crushed back against my chest for no reason other than to reassure myself she hadn't been injured, I reluctantly let her go.

Her hair pulled back in a ponytail as usual, she tucked some stray locks of dirty-blonde hair behind her ears. She blinked nervously then walked over to her phone where it was playing through a Bluetooth speaker and tapped it off.

Wiping away the divine sensation of having her body

pressed to mine for even a fleeting few seconds, I turned to the space. "Wow."

"Yeah," she laughed, "I know it looks bad, but I've got a dumpster in the back alley till Friday."

"Did you not think I'd come?"

"I knew you would," she said evenly, "but I want to do my part. I don't want you to do all the work."

Tracking back down her mostly bare, sweaty body, I then forced myself to look away and around the room. She'd managed to get two partition walls down on her own. One cubicle office.

"Give me the sledgehammer." I removed my work shirt, wearing a tight undershirt beneath, and pulled the work gloves on that I'd stuffed in my back pocket.

She handed the sledgehammer over, her eyes averted, the tips of her ears pink.

The tension that had always lived between us sizzled brighter without the buffer of her family in the room. We were rarely alone together. If so, it was me grabbing a beer out of her parents' fridge while she bustled around the kitchen. Or during holiday gatherings, when we'd accidentally bump into each other in the hallway if I went to the bathroom. Us working together—alone—on a secret project was new. Brand new.

And the sensation of having her close but wanting her closer was definitely going to drive me crazy before this was all over.

Anna turned the music back on, and I settled into work to distract myself. Smashing walls seemed to the perfect tension-breaker to keep my mind off how good she had felt pressed up against me just a minute ago.

Anna kept busy, carrying pieces of drywall out to the alley. After I'd smashed down three more cubicles, I lifted several large pieces and started hauling to the dumpster, soaking in her chipper smile as she passed me back and forth.

"So what happened to Mr. Pre-med?" I found myself asking like an idiot as I smashed down another partition.

She was standing to the side, waiting to carry the pieces I knocked down to the dumpster. I ignored the look of surprise on her face at my question. I'd never asked about her boyfriends. Had never even ragged on her like her brothers did when she brought a new one home.

That was because I didn't want to know anything about them. Didn't want to think of them making her laugh, kissing her, touching her, fucking her.

I hit the partition wall hard before glancing up at her expectantly.

"Um, he wanted me to move to New Orleans with him while he was in med school."

"You didn't want to go with him?"

She lifted one shoulder, her calm expression fixed on me. "I wanted to open a dance studio here in Beauville."

"You could've done it in New Orleans. Plenty of opportunity for a small dance studio to thrive there."

"New Orleans isn't Beauville."

I huffed out a laugh. "No. It isn't."

"Besides," she added, still holding me in her thrall, "he

wasn't what I wanted." A softening of her voice. "He wasn't the one."

A piercing sensation struck me still, hollowing me out and stealing my breath. Her pointed gaze and soft words, as well as the unspoken ones, kept me from wanting to move beyond this fragile moment of possibility.

She wasn't really saying, hinting, what I thought she was, was she?

Without a word, I nodded and picked up the sledgehammer.

After that, we worked in silence except for her music. When she turned it off, I stopped bashing at the two-by-four holding up the corner of the last cubicle.

She was tucking her phone in her back pocket when I turned to face her, my breath heaving from exertion. Her gaze wandered over my chest, that pink blush returning to her cheeks and the tips of her ears.

Fuck. If this obsession was even remotely mutual, keeping my hands off her was going to be the death of me. "You leaving?"

"Yeah. I made a spaghetti for you today, so I need to run home and get the sauce. I'll cook the noodles and bread at your place."

I was suddenly very thankful she lived in her parents' garage apartment at the moment. The last thing we needed was them asking who she cooked the spaghetti for.

"Next time, you can cook it at my place if that's easier."

Her blush darkened. She bobbed her head in agreement. "Yeah. That would probably be better. So no one…"

She didn't have to finish the sentence. We both knew that we were keeping secrets. I simply nodded.

"Okay, then. I forgot to give you your own key yesterday." She handed me what looked to be a newly cut key, her soft fingers grazing my palm. "So you won't have to wait for me to come to the studio."

Exchanging keys felt strangely intimate. I'd never given another girl a key to my house. Anna was my first. I could barely admit it to myself, but I wanted her to be the last. The only one.

"Thanks."

Then she passed close by me, leaving her hypnotic scent in her wake. "I'll get a quick shower and see you at home."

My gut tightened at both of those images. Her taking a shower to get the sweat and dirt off her slender, toned body, and her waiting for me at my home.

Fucking hell.

I was in so much fucking trouble.

Chapter Four

❦

~ANNA~

My hair was still wet when I ran up the front steps of Reed's porch. I knocked, then let myself in, knowing he was already home and expecting me.

"Reed? It's just me," I called out, but heard no answer.

I stepped through the foyer and past the hallway where I saw his bedroom door open at the end. That's when I heard the faint sound of a shower running.

Gulping hard at that mental visual, I headed straight to the kitchen and set the spaghetti sauce in the plastic container on the kitchen table. I went right to work, pulling out a pot. There was only one the right size for boiling spaghetti. It was also pristine, never-been-used. Shaking my head and smiling, I set the water to boil, then put the sauce in a larger pot, also in perfect condition, to reheat.

I'd pulled the garlic bread out of the oven and was straining the spaghetti noodles in the sink when I heard him walk into the kitchen behind me.

"Smells good, Anna."

The dark rumble of his voice stirred feelings of a different kind of hunger. When I glanced at him over my shoulder, I nearly dropped the damn noodles on the floor.

He was barefoot, wearing gray joggers and a loose, black tank, the kind he might workout in. He was also running a towel over his damp hair, drawing my attention to the flexing bulge of his biceps.

"Uh, yeah." I focused back on the spaghetti and leaned against the counter before my knees gave out. "You can have a seat."

Then I felt his body heat hovering over my left side. "You don't have to serve me. I can get it myself."

"No, it's fine." I continued shaking out the noodles though there was no water left to shake off.

He inhaled deeply then stepped back and shuffled toward the fridge. "Let's eat in front of the TV, if you don't mind. I'm beat today."

"Oh." I jerked my head around. "You want me to stay and eat?"

He paused with the fridge door open and looked at me. "I take it you haven't eaten dinner yet either, seeing how fast you made it over here." His gaze went to my wet hair then my change of shorts and T-shirt. "Having taken a shower, too."

"No, I haven't eaten."

"Then stay and eat with me." He glanced at the sauce simmering on the stove. "I can't eat all of that by myself."

I didn't mention that I'd planned on making enough for leftovers for tomorrow night. I could barely speak with him looking so fine and staring at me like that. So I nodded dumbly. "Okay then."

"What would you like to drink? I've got bottled water, Abita beer, or...bottled water."

I caught him wincing at his relatively empty fridge except for condiments, water, and beer.

"Water is fine. Thanks."

He grabbed a couple of waters, some silverware and paper towel napkins, and took them into his living room. When I made us both a plate and carried them out, I found him straightening the squares of paper towel on his coffee table and frowning. I couldn't help but smile.

"Here you go." I handed him a plate then took a seat next to him.

His frown deepened. "Maybe we should go sit at the table."

"Reed, do you normally eat dinner at the table? Or right here in front of the TV?"

Currently, his television was set on The Office reruns.

"Here."

"My job is to make your life easier, not switch things

around and complicate things. Let's eat, and then I'll get out of your hair so you can get some sleep."

With one of his tilted smiles, he leaned back into the sofa and twirled his fork in his spaghetti. I did the same but couldn't look away when he stuffed a giant bite into his mouth and closed his eyes on a pleasurable groan.

A mixture of utter bliss and tight arousal zinged down my body. "Good?" I asked hopefully.

He shook his head as he swallowed. "Fucking hell, Anna. If this is what you can do with spaghetti, I can't wait to see what else you can cook." He shot me a smile before stuffing another bite into his mouth.

A little laugh bubbled up my throat as I settled in to eat, too, strangely content with feeding him a good, tasty meal. On the TV, Jim was flirting with Pam at the reception desk. Then he quickly had to dodge away when her boyfriend Roy walked in. Jim's on-screen secret crush suddenly had sweat beading behind my neck.

Reed cleared his throat. "So what are your plans once the renovation is done?"

"What do you mean?"

"When do you plan to open the studio? And tell your parents? They're definitely going to notice the new dance studio opening on Main Street." He wiped his mouth with his napkin, having already devoured half his plate. "Everyone will."

"Actually, I was hoping we'd finish by June so I could open a summer camp in July. Then maybe offer a discount to those students for fall classes."

"That's a good idea."

His easy support was baffling and energizing. All I'd ever done since I told my parents about this idea two years ago was fight a losing battle. All they ever saw were the problems and the ways it could fail.

Reed's big, warm hand cupped my shoulder. "Hey. You okay?"

His deep voice was soft and gentle and so reassuring. I wanted to bottle that sound and swallow it whole, let it melt inside me and stay there forever.

"Yeah." I blinked away the doubts that had suddenly latched onto me with claws, trying to tear my dreams apart yet again.

"What is it?"

I'd eaten all that I could. I balled up my napkin, dropped it on the plate, then set my plate next to his on the coffee table. "It just stuns me, Reed, how much you always seem to believe in me."

When I was brave enough to look up at him, I swallowed against the unreadable expression on his face. He'd leaned sideways on the sofa, his water bottle propped on his knee, the other arm draped on the sofa back.

"It's not so hard to believe in you, Anna. You've excelled at everything you've gone after in life."

I huffed out a laugh. "But I've doubted myself every step of the way."

His frown returned. "Why?"

I turned more toward him, crooking my knee on the sofa so I could face him, holding my water bottle with both hands in my lap. "I think being the baby sister was part of it."

He was quiet and waited. That was one thing I'd always adored about Reed. In a family that was tumultuous and too loud by nature, he was always the calm one amongst the storm. And such a good listener. He put me at ease, well, when he wasn't making me sweat with his insane hotness.

"They've always been so protective," I added. "My parents, my brothers. But more than that, they've always pushed me to be better."

"And that's a bad thing?"

Smiling, I admitted, "No. And yes." I shrugged a shoulder, tearing at the paper label on the water bottle. "It's like my best was never quite good enough. I'm not saying they weren't always proud of me. They were. Some of the pressure came from myself. But…"

"But?"

"Okay, so remember that summer I was trying to learn to do the backflip off the diving board."

Reed clenched his jaw, and the fingers of his hand on the back of the sofa curled. "I remember." His voice had dropped deeper.

"Jonah and Justin kept giving me pointers until, finally, I did it. I remember the day, specifically, because it was right before I left for dance camp. So when I finally did it, you know what Jonah said?"

He shook his head, his gaze intense, his focus riveted on me.

"He said, 'Good job, Anna Banana, now you need to learn how to do a somersault.'" I scoffed. "I know he meant well, but it always felt like my achievements, great or small, were never enough. And it just jars me when you"—I gestured toward him— "are just you."

I let out the hundredth nervous laugh of the day, staring at my lap. The hand he had on the sofa back lowered to my bare knee, and he gave it a squeeze.

"Your family loves you beyond reason, Anna. They may not be the greatest at supporting you unconditionally, but they believe in you."

"Not like you," I practically whispered, snagging his gaze.

In the dim light of the television, his midnight-blue eyes darkened to stormy gray. The intimate quiet of his living room felt suddenly small and oppressive. Not with something terrible and crushing, but with heady emotion and tight anticipation.

I didn't miss the way Reed's heated gaze dropped to my mouth or the growing warmth of his big hand enveloping my knee. Scowling, he blinked and pulled his hand away, like he hadn't realized what he was doing.

He picked up our plates and stood. "I'll take care of the dishes. Dinner was delicious."

"Oh, sure." I popped up and followed him into the kitchen where I'd set my purse.

He roughly scraped the scraps from my plate into the garbage and then put the plate in the sink. There was nothing left on his, which again sent a bubble of joy through me.

"Well, I'll do my first cleaning tomorrow while you're at work. I can put this spaghetti away for tomorrow's dinner."

"No, I've got it," he quickly said, turning toward me with a hand on the sink. "I'll put this away for tomorrow."

"I didn't have time to do a salad, but I can make you one for tomorrow night."

He watched me with those keen eyes, the tip of his mouth curling up like I loved so much. That look always lightened the mood and eased the tension that seemed to constantly build between us.

"You don't have to. This is better than anything I've eaten since last time I went to Nana's."

I laughed and pulled my purse over my shoulder. "Good." I nodded emphatically. "Tomorrow then."

"I'll walk you out."

"I don't think I'll get attacked in the driveway, Reed."

His scowl returned full-force. "I'll walk you out," he repeated, voice deepening to something dangerous, the lightness of a second ago vanishing.

I turned and walked ahead of him, wondering what had set him off. Then, automatically, my thoughts raced to that time long ago where I *had* been attacked in a driveway. The time that he'd saved me.

That was the first secret he'd kept for me. He'd never told Jonah. Never told a soul.

When I walked down the steps into the evening heat, I turned. "Thanks again, Reed. For everything."

Rather than answer, he simply nodded and watched me all the way to my car, arms crossed. He was still watching on his porch when I backed out onto the main road and drove away.

Only when I was finally out of sight did my muscles relax and the tension ease. It had always been that way between us. While I couldn't ever seem to make the discomforting tightness go away, it didn't compel me to leave his company. The opposite, actually.

It was like that feeling you get on a roller coaster when you're climbing that first steep incline. Your stomach is tight, butterflies are building, and your nerves are bearing down and getting you ready for the exciting big drop. That's how I felt every time I was with Reed. Except we never got to the big drop. Not yet anyway.

But a girl could dream.

Chapter Five

❧

~REED~

As I drove home from Anna's studio around eight, I was still working out how to get Hale to help me on this job for her without spilling her secret to Jonah. I'd finished gutting it this week, including the carpets, but I'd need professional help to put down the hardwood floors.

Jonah and I had known Hale since high school. And afterwards, when he'd started his construction company with nothing but an inexperienced crew of buddies looking to make an extra buck, we were in on it.

While Jonah left for college and only came home to help work on Hale's crew during summers, I'd stayed on and worked my way up to become his first foreman. His company expanded quickly so that I was in charge of my own crew, building mostly residential houses in newer neighborhoods in Beauville and towns nearby.

Hale was more my friend, as well as my boss, than Jonah's, but that didn't mean he wouldn't love to cause trouble by telling Jonah what I was doing. Hale was a natural-born shit-stirrer.

The other problem with telling him was risking the high probability that he'd wonder why I was doing this for Anna. Would he think I was doing it because I had feelings for her? Feelings I shouldn't be having for my best friend's baby sister? Because he'd be right.

When Anna had shown up on my back porch that late afternoon with hope in her pretty eyes, I knew that whatever she wanted from me, I was going to give it to her.

It felt like I'd been trying my whole damn life to suppress what I felt for her. But it had really started the night I'd saved her from that party and from that asshole, Blake Guidry, when she was in high school. Even today, I'd get raging mad thinking about that night and what could've happened to her. It had changed things between us.

Yes, I'd noticed like any red-blooded male that she was growing into a beautiful, sexy young woman. But there was something about that night, specifically, that had set my mind on a different, very non-brotherly course where Anna was concerned. I'd started thinking about her as mine to protect. More than Jonah's or her other brothers or even her father's.

Which was ridiculous.

She wasn't mine, nor was she meant to be. Which is why I'd worked as late as possible this past week on her studio, not wanting her to be there when I got home. The temptation of having her alone in my house was too much for me to bear. I was only mortal.

That's why I was pretty shocked—and somewhat panicked—to find her car still sitting in the driveway when I pulled up. When I walked through the back door into the laundry room, I knew for sure that fate was fucking with me.

Anna was bent over the dryer, pulling my towels, work shirts, and goddamn boxer briefs out and dropping them into a basket. It wasn't her handling my underwear that made a hot surge flood south of my belt. It was those tiny shorts she was wearing again, revealing so much of what I wanted to touch, kiss...bite.

"Working a little late," I mumbled too gruffly as I weaved around her and into the kitchen.

Whatever she'd cooked smelled amazing, my stomach growling instantly.

"Hey! Yeah." She walked into the kitchen, laundry basket in hand. "You're working late too," she added softly.

I stared at her, standing in my kitchen in flip-flops, a tank top, and cut-offs, her hair in a messy bun, no make-up, and a stain on her shirt, likely from cooking my dinner. A rush of heavy, powerful emotion left me breathless.

I wanted this to be real, not an exchange of services. I wanted Anna Hebert waiting for me when I got home, flitting around my house like it was her own. I wanted her scent in the air, in my sheets, on my skin. I wanted that look she was giving me now to be the prelude to me pulling her into my arms and sinking my hands into her hair, my tongue into her mouth.

I simply wanted *Anna*.

The intensity of it had never barreled over and crushed me the way it was right now as she blew an errant, stray lock of hair out of her eyes. The same eyes gazing at me with both trepidation and something much more like desire.

Warning alarms blared in my head.

Clearing my throat, I broke the spell and turned to the stove where I picked up the lid on a cast iron skillet. "Dinner smells good."

"Let me put these down, and I'll make you a plate."

"Go sit down, and I'll make us both a plate."

She blinked in surprise but didn't reply as she disappeared into the living room. I dished out the chicken and rice casserole onto two plates, then some green beans cooked down with bacon and onions from the other pot on the stove.

"I made some iced tea today, so I'll get that," she added, walking back into the kitchen and reaching up for two glasses from the cabinet next to me.

Unable to help myself, I watched, savoring the brief

sight of skin on her stomach when her shirt rode up. "You know you could've just bought some iced tea."

"Yeah, but I know how you love my Mom's home-brewed sweet tea. I don't mind making it for you."

I blew out a sharp breath and carried our plates into the living room. "You're going to spoil me so much that I won't want to let you go when this job is done."

She followed me and sat down on the sofa beside me, placing the glasses on coasters that I didn't even know I had.

"I can continue cooking and cleaning for you after the job is done," she offered, again in that soft, shy voice that made me want to kiss the fuck out of her, then bite her. Her sweetness had a tendency to call to my most primitive instincts, and I couldn't fucking understand it.

Damn, my aggression was overkill when it came to her. This was dangerous. She made me want to do things to her, not giving a good goddamn what my best friend or anyone else would think about it. She made me forget everything but her.

I sat back with my plate in my lap and picked up the remote. "What do you want to watch tonight?"

The first suggestion that popped up on screen when I opened Netflix was the new season of *The Witcher*.

"Ooo, let's watch that," she said excitedly.

"I haven't seen the first season."

"*What?*" She sat up straighter. "How can you not have seen this yet?"

I remembered that she loved reading fantasy novels. Of course, this would be her thing.

"I prefer documentaries." I shoveled some rice and chicken into my mouth, grunting at how good it was.

"Serial killer and murder documentaries, sure. But none of that can compare to *The Witcher*."

"You watch murder documentaries?"

"Yes…and?" She sipped her tea, eyeing me.

"Doesn't seem like something you'd like."

She arched a dark blond brow and set her glass down. "There are lots of things you don't know about me, sir." Her voice had fallen into a silky register that made my dick twitch. Especially when she called me *sir*. "I have layers."

Tamping down the primitive thoughts I was having, I asked, "What's so intriguing about *The Witcher*?"

"The books are better than the show, but I love both." Her mouth quirked into a smile, and her expression turned thoughtful. "First off, the writing is brilliant. And the monsters the author creates are unique, even compared to so many other fantasy books I've read."

"Why do you like fantasy books so much?" I asked, finishing off my plate.

She swallowed a bite, brows scrunching up. "I think it's the pure escape into another world that feels so real. Where there are villains and heroes and impossible magic. But really, I love the unique and magical worlds, and just being a part of it for a while."

"So you read to escape?"

"Not completely."

"But partly."

"Yes." Her brown eyes were dark and impenetrable in the dim light.

"What do you need to escape from?" Concern pinched my chest. "Is something wrong?"

Her pensive look lightened suddenly with a laugh, a sound that rippled straight to my heart. "Nothing's wrong," she assured me. "I have a good family and a good life. I have nothing to complain about." Her gaze dropped.

"But?"

Her eyes lifted. "I always feel this pressure." She placed a hand over her sternum, her plate still in her lap. "It's not necessarily my parents. Or my brothers. But sometimes, it is. I feel this need to be *more* or to be perfect or to be whatever it is they think I'm supposed to be."

You are perfect nearly fell from my lips. I bit back those words but couldn't let it rest at that. "Anna, your family only pushes you because they love you."

"I know that." She let out a sigh. "I know that. But it doesn't make the pressure any less. Or the feelings of... inadequacy go away."

"Inadequacy?" My shock was evident in my voice.

Her gaze found mine again, expression wondering.

"There are so many words to describe you, Anna, but inadequate is not one of them."

She now held her plate by the sides, perched on her lap, her dinner forgotten. "What words would you use to describe me?"

Dangerous. So dangerous.

Still, I told her. "Courageous. Talented. Intelligent."

Her cheeks washed with pink as her eyes widened further.

"Beautiful," I added softly.

So fucking beautiful my heart ached when I looked at her.

Her mouth was ajar, her chest rising and falling more rapidly. She licked her lips, then said, "I'm not perfect."

"No," I agreed. "You can be headstrong and willful beyond reason. Sometimes impulsive."

Rather than react with hurt, her mouth broke wide and she laughed again, rewarding me with more of that sweet, hypnotic sound.

"And don't forget dramatic," she added, "as my mother always says."

"I'd call it passionate rather than dramatic."

And just like that, the electric tension constricted like a tight rope stretching between us.

Needing to get away from this topic before I fell on my knees like a smitten schoolboy and swore my love to her, I added playfully, "So *The Witcher* is a good escape, but I'd say you like it for another reason."

"What's that?" she asked, smiling.

"I'm pretty sure most women like it for the star of the show, Henry Cavill."

She blushed but added brightly, "Why wouldn't I?"

"I figured." I chuckled. "So you're a Cavill fan too?"

"Yeah, I like a big, thick man."

She sat, facing forward, her plate perched on her knees. But I didn't miss her side glance that became less of a glance and more of a lingering look down my body, stalling at my chest and thighs.

Forcing myself to keep my breathing steady and even, I kept focused on the TV and flicked on episode one of the show. I could hardly believe it, but Anna Hebert was checking me out.

After she finished eating, I took her plate and brought both of ours to the sink. When I returned, she was sitting sideways with her back on the other end of the sofa, her knees up. I settled back onto my side.

I could barely focus on the show because Anna had let her feet slide forward till the tips of her toes touched my hip. By the time the episode ended, her toes were neatly tucked beneath my thigh.

The thing was, this would've been totally normal had we been at her parents' house, all of us watching a movie together in the living room. Casual touches had been commonplace when she was growing up. It had still tortured me then, but I'd accepted my role as her surrogate brother. Mostly.

But now, in the quiet isolation of my own living room, it felt achingly intimate. And her sultry looks and suggestive banter had tied my stomach into knots and had my cock rock-hard.

I was thankful when the episode ended. I quickly stood and clicked the TV off. "I need to call it a night."

"Sure." She popped up, nervousness in her voice. "Of course. Sorry."

"No apologies needed. Thank you for dinner."

"You don't have to thank me." She picked up her purse and headed for the front door. "Just doing my job."

I followed her toward the front door. "Still, I appreciate it."

Our exchanges were stiff and cordial and not like us at all. That electric sizzle simmered below the surface so we both reverted to polite talk to cover what was brewing beneath.

She turned to face me, putting her back to the door. "And I appreciate you."

That look. That voice. I wasn't imagining or fantasizing this into reality. Anna wanted me.

I held myself rigid, unable to move or speak, fisting my hands at my sides so I wouldn't reach for her. If I touched her, it would all be over.

Then she stood up away from the door. When I thought she would turn and let herself out, she stepped closer to me instead, her dark eyes wide but determined.

"Anna." My warning was low and gruff, my self-discipline shredding to nothing.

She didn't step back or flinch away. She reached out with her hand and pressed it over my dirty T-shirt I still hadn't changed out of. Her small hand lay over my heart, which was trying to pound straight through my chest and into her palm.

"Reed," she whispered, those sweet eyes gazing up at me with a daring plea shining bright in them.

"Fuck," I mumbled then I cupped her face and crushed my mouth to hers.

A whimper escaped her mouth before I swallowed it and stroked her tongue with mine. I'd always imagined that Anna needed a man to be gentle and tender with her, but I wasn't that man. I couldn't be. A lifetime of lust and obsession and knee-buckling adoration burst forth in that kiss.

Pushing her back to the door, I crushed my chest to hers, relishing the feel of her small breasts flush against me. A rumble vibrated up my throat as I nipped at her lower lip with teeth then licked to soothe it.

"Oh, God," she breathed when I closed my fist around her bun and tugged her head back, exposing the silken skin of her throat.

Skating away from her mouth, I nipped her jaw then trailed my tongue down her neck, kissing my way back to her ear. "You taste like fucking heaven, Anna."

She wrapped a knee over my hip, thrusting her pelvis into mine. Without a thought, I gripped the bare thigh of her other leg and hauled her up till her pussy sat right on top of the raging hard-on pushing against my zipper.

Still fisting her hair, I angled her head so that I could slant my mouth over hers and go deep, grinding my dick against the heat of her. I was losing my mind.

Anna clawed at my hair with one hand, the other slipping under my shirt so she could mark me with her blunt nails. I rocked against her in a mimicry of fucking, let her feel the evidence of what she did to me, my mind hazed with white-hot lust. She scraped a nail across my nipple.

Hissing, I gripped the strap of her tank top and bra and then yanked them both off her shoulder, her perfect, pink-tipped breast popping free. On a savage sound, I lowered my head and wrapped my mouth over most of her breast, sucking till I got to the tip, letting my teeth drag over the tight peak.

"Reed!" she cried, her legs tightening around my waist as she ground against me, seeking her release.

I tightened my grip in her hair, my other hand pinching her reddened nipple. Then I cupped her breast with my hand so that her perfect center pointed closer to my mouth. I flicked the sensitive tip with my tongue as her cries grew more frantic, louder. Relentlessly, I tongued and nipped and sucked and ground her against the door.

"Please, oh, God, I'm going to come."

I straightened, holding my mouth against hers but not kissing, just circling my thumb and flicking her nipple. Her eyes were squeezed closed, her mouth ajar as she rode my jean-covered dick.

"Look at me, baby."

Her eyes shot open, the brown swallowed by the black of her blissed-out pupils.

"Yeah, let me see you when you come." I rocked harder against her, dragging between her sweet thighs, brain completely gone for this girl. "Come for me, Anna," I whispered against her mouth, saying words aloud I'd only ever done in my own fantasies.

Then she cried out and spasmed in my arms. I pressed her tight against the door and swallowed her orgasmic moans, delving deep with my tongue, tasting the sweet ecstasy of her trembling with a climax. One *I'd* given her.

I mounded her breast possessively, holding her, pinning her to the door still, wishing I'd had the patience to strip her bare and bury my cock so deep she'd never forget who made her come this hard.

I flinched at where my mind had gone and broke the kiss. Anna's head was tilted back into the cradle of my hand that had never let her go. Like a goddamn caveman, I'd held her still while I'd nearly fucked her against the door. I would have had she not been so responsive, had she not come so fast that it brought me back to the reality of what had just happened.

Her eyes were mere slits of post-orgasm euphoria, her swollen lips parted and panting. Anna's breast was still gripped in my sun-dark, calloused hand.

What the fuck had I done?

Righting her bra strap and tank, I gripped her hips and lowered her to the floor. She wobbled back, so I held her upright. Her hands rested on my shoulders.

"Anna, I—"

"Don't say you shouldn't have done that."

The fierce tenor of her voice grabbed my attention. "I shouldn't have."

"Because of Jonah?"

I couldn't respond because she said it so fiercely, like it was absurd that we'd let something like Jonah stop us. If I'd thought there was a chance of Anna wanting more with me than sex, then I'd argue the same. But I wasn't sure about that.

I wasn't an idiot. I knew Anna had had a schoolgirl crush on me years ago, but she'd moved on to better pastures and dated the kind of guy she truly wanted to marry in college. All of her boyfriends had been well-educated, white-collar types. I was the exact opposite.

If I thought she could relieve her pent-up lust for a rough-handed man on me and then walk away without a broken heart, yeah, I'd be all for this. And again, if she wasn't a woman I'd be forced to see for years and years to come after she'd settle down with a lawyer or doctor or whoever-the-fuck and have her perfect kids and her perfect life then I'd yet again be saying, *let's do this.*

But I was pretty positive that Anna was at a crossroads in life where she was finding herself and her place in this world. Experimentation came with the territory. Why not have a fling with the guy she'd crushed on as a young girl? Before she settled into a real life with another man. That's what this was.

I stepped away from her. "This can't happen."

She winced, and I gritted my teeth against the pain flickering in her dark eyes. She swallowed hard and tilted her chin higher. "I see."

She pulled the door open behind her, still staring at me, a defiance in her gaze I'd seen a million times before when her family had told her she didn't know what she was doing.

"Goodnight then, Reed."

She walked out with a sharp sway to her step and left me there with a suffocating pain squeezing my chest.

If this was me saving myself from heartbreak, then why did it hurt so goddamn bad?

Chapter Six

~ANNA~

"He's an idiot," said my best friend.

Emma Mouton sat next to me at the bar of the Drunk Pelican where we'd been drinking for the past hour.

"Not every guy wants a woman like me," I told her, having just confessed to her everything that had happened last night at Reed's.

"What the hell kind of nonsense is that? What kind of woman do you mean? Beautiful? Smart? Kind?"

Rolling my eyes, I sipped my lemon drop martini. "I'm also flighty and impulsive. Reed is solid and grounded. He doesn't get hair-brained ideas like sinking his life savings into a building that needs serious renovation when there aren't enough funds to finish the job."

"He agreed to do the renovations, so it doesn't look like he thinks it's crazy."

"That's because Reed would never say so. He's too... Reed." I tipped back and finished my drink.

"Another round, ladies?"

The bartender, Margot, was a striking brunette with a full sleeve tattoo up her right arm, silver studs up one ear, and a tiny diamond piercing in her nose. She radiated badass vibes. She wore her hair twisted in a messy bun, and her green feline-shaped eyes were intense and watchful just like an actual cat. She wasn't from Beauville, and I didn't know her story, but she'd been working at the Drunk Pelican at least two years. She always had a polite smile and kind word for those at the bar.

"Maybe one more," said Emma before I could answer.

"I should probably go home and wallow in my misery with ice cream and Netflix."

"No, you don't want to do that yet."

"Why not?"

Emma nudged my elbow. When I looked at her, she pointed her chin toward the entrance.

A host of butterflies burst in my stomach at the sight of the three men sauntering in the door. My brother Jonah was first, followed by Hale, then Reed. His hard gaze landed on me instantly and never left.

They eased through the small crowd. The Drunk Pelican had all kinds of fun theme nights, trivia, and improv and stuff. But tonight was just booze and a steady stream of country music.

"Hey, Anna Banana," called Jonah, his smirky smile all for Emma as he put a hand on the backs of both of our chairs. He wasn't even looking at me.

"Hey, Jonah." I spun all the way around to face him, knocking his arm off. "You boys carousing on a Saturday night?" I kept my eyes off Reed, though I felt his on me.

Hale crowded me on my other side, a hand propped on the bar. "Looking good there, Hebert." He checked out my cleavage, which was revealed quite a bit by the low V-neck blouse I was wearing. "Let me get you another one of those fruity drinks."

"Ease up, Broussard," said Jonah. "Hands and eyes off my sister."

Hale laughed, but I caught his gaze on Reed, not on my brother. That's when I was finally brave enough to let myself look at Reed. He had both hands in his pockets, his jaw clenched and his scowl deadly fierce on Hale.

Margot set two more lemon drop martinis in front of me and Emma, which caught Hale's attention. Of course, every pretty girl caught Hale's attention.

"What can I get you guys?" she asked Jonah. My brother was a regular here.

"Heineken?" he asked, glancing over his shoulder.

Reed shrugged, still looking murderous.

"Three Heinekens. Thanks, Margot."

"Who's she?" asked Hale, still crowding me on my right.

"Margot," said Jonah with sarcasm.

"No shit. I meant, where's she been? I've never seen her."

"She's been working here a while," my brother answered. "Maybe you should get out more."

"Some of us actually work for a living," Hale shot back.

Jonah laughed, never caring what anyone thought of his current employment status. He'd finished his General Studies degree years ago and then worked for a pipeline company who made pipes for offshore oil rigs for five years. Until last year at Christmas dinner when he promptly announced that he'd quit his job and was writing his first novel.

Dad had asked how he'd pay bills, but he'd apparently saved quite a bit from the oil field company. When we'd asked what he was writing, he said he'd tell us when he was done. Since then, he'd rented a small duplex in town and was apparently writing a novel.

I was one of the few who didn't hassle him about his unconventional decision to quit a good-paying job and throw caution to the wind. I knew what it felt like when people squashed your dreams. Or tried to.

When Margot delivered their beers, Hale caught her attention and asked her something I couldn't hear.

"Pretty dress, Emma," said my not-so-subtle brother, easing closer to her after taking a sip of his beer. "You going to dance with me tonight?"

"Would you stop hitting on my best friend, Jonah?" I complained.

But Emma gave him a flirty smile, which she never *ever*

did, then winked at me. "Hell, yeah, Hebert. Let's go." She hopped down off the stool, grabbed his hand, and hauled him off to the small dancefloor.

She was playing wingman—or wing-woman rather—but that only had my nerves spiking even more. Reed hadn't moved, simply stood there, fuming and drinking his beer.

Margot headed back to help customers, so Hale turned sideways to me, standing really close. I was still facing away from the bar on my stool.

"So," Hale tugged on my ponytail, "how about you finally give me a dance, Anna Banana?"

I was trying to figure out a way to put him down nicely when Reed made a rude growling noise and shoved Hale backward a step before he planted his hands on my waist and lifted me off the stool onto my feet.

"Not on your fucking life," he grumbled to one of his best friends who happened to be his boss.

Hale barked out a laugh and winked at me just like Emma had before gulping his beer. Like they were all in on the same joke. Reed grabbed my hand and tugged me through the crowded bar, maneuvering us to the opposite side of the dancefloor of Jonah and Emma.

He pulled me aggressively into his arms, one hand on my hip, the other on the small of my back, keeping me close. I didn't even know this slow country song, but my body was all for it even though my heart was throwing up red flags.

My hands on his shoulders, I glanced up to find him still wearing that deep frown. "Why are you so mad?"

"I don't like Hale flirting with you."

Rolling my eyes, I snort-laughed. "You've been scowling like a grumpy bear since you walked in, and Hale is always flirty. He has no other setting."

"I didn't like finding you in the bar either," he admitted, turning us slowly so that we were more in the shadow of the corner.

"Reed. What's your problem? I'm having drinks with my friend. And it's not like you have a say-so in my life."

He held me tighter, his hand on my waist sliding to my hip. "What if I wanted a say-so in your life?"

"Are you kidding me right now? Last night, you said"—I gestured between us—"*this* can't happen. I clearly remember."

He winced, but his hold on me didn't ease for a second. "What I want is different from what we actually *can* do."

"Do you see me as a child or something?"

He huffed out a sad laugh. "No." He shook his head so emphatically that a wayward lock of dark hair fell into his eyes.

"Hey, Reed!" Jonah and Emma twirled by us. Reed tensed. "Keep your hands higher, bro, or I'll have to break them."

Then they whirled away, which was weird because it was a slow song. Then again, my brother was weird.

Reed sighed but didn't move his hands from where

he'd already had them—low and tight on my body. If anything, he clenched me closer.

"You afraid of my brother?"

He looked away. "It's not that. Not really."

"So if it isn't my brother, then what?"

He kept silent, clenching that perfectly square jaw, which only gave me thoughts of kissing and biting it and then down his muscular throat.

"You won't even tell me why?"

Jaw clenching, he finally looked down at me, his expression a mixture of anger and frustration. "Anna, I don't want to have casual sex with someone I've known my whole life and will likely know the rest of my life."

"Who says I want *casual* sex?"

If possible, his body coiled tighter, flexing and gathering me infinitesimally closer. Then the scowl returned with a vengeance.

"I'm not your type for anything but a casual fuck. And trust me"—his voice dropped to a rusty, gravelly tone —"there's nothing more I'd like to do than fuck you good and hard. But you'd regret it the second you brought your next boyfriend home."

I scoffed. "Now you're telling me what I want and how I'd feel?"

"I know you, Anna."

"Not well enough," I snapped, because this jerk had no idea that I'd compared every single guy I'd ever dated to him. And when each one of them fell short because they never looked at me the way Reed did or spoke to me the way he did, like I mattered, like my thoughts and beliefs and dreams mattered, I ended up letting them go.

"What do you mean?" he barked back.

"I mean you're an idiot." I pushed out of his arms and stormed my way through the crowd toward the bar where I'd left my purse hanging on the bar stool.

Jonah was laughing with Hale and Emma about something. I quickly screwed on my happy face so my brother wouldn't detect anything.

"Em, I need to get going." I grabbed my purse and strapped it on my shoulder. "I totally forgot I've got to help a friend with this thing tomorrow."

I was lying, but Jonah didn't seem to notice. Oblivious, that one.

"Sure," said Emma. "No problem. Let's get going."

"So soon?" whined Jonah to Emma. "Come on, Anna. Don't be a drag on a Saturday night."

Emma read the warning loud and clear. "You can try unsuccessfully to get into my pants another night, Hebert," she told him before giving him a rough pat on the face.

"Promise?" he practically begged.

"Gross, Jonah." I scowled at him then waved to Hale who was looking over my shoulder. I didn't even make eye contact with Reed who'd made his way back to our group. "Come on, Em."

I led the way and blew out a heavy breath as we strolled toward the car parked on the street.

"Wanna talk about it?" she asked.

"No." If I did, I'd cry.

Reed thought I was only good for casual sex? He didn't want to pursue something because of the awkward discomfort of having to see me afterward? An empty hole was opening up somewhere in the center of my chest, and I didn't know how to keep it from cracking me in half.

"He's an idiot," said Emma.

"I told him so."

"You did?" She wrapped an arm around my shoulders, squeezed me close, and kissed my temple. "So proud of you."

That made me laugh as we walked down the sidewalk with our arms around each other.

"Thank you for leaving with me so suddenly without asking anything."

"Of course. Sisters before misters, you know that."

"I love you."

"Love you, too."

"You don't really want to sleep with my brother, do you?"

It was her turn to laugh. "No, Anna Banana."

I pinched her hip where I had my arm draped. She knew I hated that nickname.

"Don't worry," she assured me. "Your brother's hot, but I'm not going there. Plenty of other snakes in the garden."

"I thought it was fish in the sea."

"Not when it comes to your brother. He's a big, wicked snake. And probably *has* a big snake." She waggled her eyebrows suggestively.

"Ew." I pushed her away. "Please don't talk about my brother's...snake."

Just like always, Emma had me laughing and cackling all the way home. It wasn't until my head was on my pillow that I let the heartache bloom a bit more, spreading a sadness I wasn't sure I'd ever be able to fully let go.

Chapter Seven

~REED~

"So are we going to talk about it?" asked Hale as we worked on the final section of hardwood flooring.

"Nope."

"You finally went for it, and she turned you down?"

I gave him an eat-shit look and fitted another plank of the pale oak flooring into place, tapping lightly with the hammer.

"Or Jonah found out and beat the shit out of you since Saturday," he guessed.

Sighing, I sat back on my heels. "No. Jonah doesn't know. And I didn't get turned down." I picked up another plank out of the box next to me. "Not exactly."

"This is awesome. What does that mean?"

"I told her Saturday that it couldn't happen. I mean, it's pointless, right?"

"No. Why would it be?" He leaned over and held the next plank in place, both of us working in tandem as we had the last few hours.

Fortunately, when I asked Hale to do me this favor and keep it from Jonah, he agreed a lot faster than I thought he would with very few questions. He even suggested we knock off early from a residential job to get the flooring done here in one day.

I thought he was just being generous, but now I knew he was trying to invade my personal life. I could hardly pretend that I wasn't doing this job partially because of my feelings for Anna. Besides, I had no one to talk to about it, seeing as my best friend was part of the whole damn problem.

"Why would it be pointless?" he asked again.

"Anna's younger. She's still playing the field."

"Anna Hebert?" he asked with obvious surprise. "That girl's been too serious her whole damn life. I can't see her suddenly wanting to sow some oats and sleep around."

"Maybe not." The tight knot in my gut refused to loosen. "But I'm not the kind of guy she usually dates. She likes college boys. Her type is...not me."

"Funny, because she broke up with all of those other college boys, right?" He didn't wait for an answer as he hammered the next plank into place. "If she's open to seeing where this goes, then you should listen to her." He sat back on his heels, giving me a heavy look, which wasn't Hale's norm. "She's worth the risk, isn't she?"

Anna? She was worth everything. I suddenly felt stupid. If I knew that she wanted me for more than a night, I'd fight Jonah and his brothers and anyone else for the chance to be with her.

She'd even insinuated the other night that what she wanted was more than casual sex. The knot in my gut tightened. I'd pushed her away because I was afraid.

Standing, I combed both hands through my hair and laced my fingers behind my head as I looked out, noticing the sun had set since we'd gotten here.

"Fuck." I looked at Hale still on the floor. "I'm a goddamn idiot."

"If you gave up on Anna before it even started, then yeah, you are."

"Fuck!"

I glanced at my watch. She might still be at the house, though she'd made a point all week to be finished and gone by the time I got home around eight. It was close to seven now.

"Go on." He grinned. "I'll finish and lock up."

"Thanks, man." I quickly pulled the key off my keychain and handed it over, then jetted out the door. I was pulling into my drive ten minutes later, cursing because her car was gone.

Still, I rushed inside, somehow hoping she'd miraculously be there. A delicious smelling dinner covered in foil waited on the stove. My kitchen and living room were swept and mopped clean, my clothes dried and folded in a laundry basket beside the sofa. She'd never invaded my bedroom and put things away.

Pulling out my phone, I texted her.

ME: Hey. Where are you?

It was read almost immediately, and the little ellipses of her typing back hovered for several minutes before a message came through.

ANNA: None of your biness.

What the hell? Did she mean *business*? Then another one.

ANNA: I don't have to tell you where I'm at. I did my job. Made yur favorite dinner to.

This was weird. The few times she'd texted me before to ask where the Windex or my cutting board was, before realizing I didn't own such things, she'd always been polite with perfect grammar. Her texts were just like her, sweet and perfect. But these weren't. Something was off.

I hit dial and waited. She answered on the second ring. The sound of people laughing and a loud crowd in the background had me frowning.

"Where are you?" I asked without saying hello.

"I told you, *Reeeed*. None of your business."

Yep. There was a slight slur to her words.

Then I heard a voice on a mic in the background saying that round two went to Team Fellowship of the Ring. I realized it was Thursday night, trivia night at the Drunk Pelican.

"Stay there, Anna. I'm on my way."

She was still mouthing off to me when I hung up and hurried for my truck, hightailing it back across town. I'd been minutes from her on Main Street when I left Hale at her studio. Someone was pulling out of a parking spot along the street as I pulled up. I parallel parked then rushed into the bar, still wearing my dirty work clothes and not giving two fucks about it.

Most of the crowd was separated at tables around the stage where the MC was calling out questions. I instantly found Anna at the bar talking to Margot. She was wearing a short summer dress very similar to the one she wore at the last family barbeque. It was loose and showed entirely too much skin and had my fingers itching.

I nodded to Margot as I stepped up. She had both elbows on the bar, forearms folded together as she listened to whatever Anna was saying.

"You Reed?" she asked.

"Yeah."

"Glad you're here. She's going to need a ride home."

Anna swiveled on her barstool, her legs crossed, giving me a superior look, her nose tipped in the air, her eyes glazed. "Don't know if I wanna ride home from him. Em was s'posed to come."

Margot shook her head and said to me, "She's been drinking martinis for a while now. I cut her off, but I think her friend is a no-show."

"Come on, Anna." I offered a hand to help her down. "Let's get going."

"Don't need your help, *Reed*," she sassed, which didn't sting nearly as much with her slurred speech.

But when she hopped down from the stool, she slipped on her sandal. I grabbed her around the waist then scooped her into my arms.

"What do I owe you?" I asked Margot.

She waved me off. "Just get her home safely. As much as she's been talking my ear off about how mad at you she is, I'd say you're the one she wants to take care of her."

The thought of being the one to take care of her, the one she wanted, had my heart racing.

"Thank you," I told Margot and made my way to the door.

Margot opened it for me. The trivia guests never noticed a thing since they were so focused on the next question about who was Deadpool's favorite taxi driver.

Anna mumbled something I didn't hear, her head turned into my shoulder, her arms around my neck. When the noise died down out on the street, I realized she was sniffing my shirt.

"Damn, why do you smell so good?" she asked, burying her nose in my nasty work shirt.

"Anna," I laughed. "I smell like sweat and dirt."

"No, no, no." She shook her head, glassy eyes looking up at me. "You smell like heaven. Sometimes, when I'm at your house, I want to steal a bunch of your clothes, take them home, spread them on my bed, and roll around on them."

"Uh." I didn't know what to say to that, but it was somehow making me hard.

What the hell was happening?

"Naked," she added, trailing a finger along my jaw. "I wanna roll in them naked."

Fuck me.

"Why is your jaw so perfect?"

"You're drunk, sweetheart."

"Yeah. But you know what? When you're drunk, it only makes you say the things you wanna say but won't because of natural inbihitions. I mean, inhibitions." She giggled, her head lolling against my chest as I stepped up to my truck.

After setting her on her feet, I opened the door and managed to get her in the seat and belted easily enough. Once back in the driver's seat, I pulled out and headed toward her house, which was in the opposite direction of mine.

"No, no, no! Please, Reed, please, please don't take me home. I'm already a disappointment to my parents. I don't wanna 'splain why I'm drunk."

We sat at a red light.

"Please, Reed." She reached her hand over and set it on my thigh.

Tensing, I took her hand, squeezed it, and placed it back in her lap before I took a right at the light and headed back toward my house.

"Why are you drunk, Anna?"

"Emma stood me up." She raised her hands and

flopped them back on her lap. "What else was I s'posed to do?"

"Go back home and not get drunk by yourself," I suggested.

"Yeah, but I wanted to get drunk. I wanted to not think so much." She leaned her forehead against the window. "I'm always thinking too much," she whispered, drawing something with her finger on the glass where she'd fogged it up with her breath.

"What are you always thinking about?" I asked gently.

"You."

Then she heaved a sigh, and my heart hammered so hard against my ribcage, I thought it was trying to come right out of my chest.

"Me?" I swallowed hard.

"Yeah. It's so sad really." She laughed, but there was more sorrow than joy in it. "Pathetic is what I am. You don't want me."

"That's not what I said, Anna." I stopped at a red light and looked over at her.

Fuck, I should not be arguing with her while she was drunk. She probably wouldn't even remember this.

"You said you wanted a casual fuck." Then she unbelted her buckle.

"What are you doing? Put your seatbelt back on."

But she ignored me and crawled across the bench seat. She kneeled on one knee and draped the other leg over mine. She had one hand on my chest, the other in my hair, tugging on the strands at the back of my neck.

Fucking hell. What did I do to deserve this?

"Anna," I warned in a gruff tone, but her eyes were on my mouth, and she wasn't in the least bit threatened. "Go sit down and put on your seat belt."

The light turned green, but I wasn't moving. I was trying not to lose my mind.

"I can do casual sex, Reed, if that's all you want."

"Anna, please go sit down." *For the love of everything holy, go sit back fucking down and get your sweet, beautiful ass back in your seat.*

"What did you say? That you'd like to fuck me good and hard?"

She was practically in my lap, and my dick was a stone pipe in my pants, but there was no goddamn way I was touching her in this state.

Then she sat on my right thigh, the heat of her pussy soaking through my jeans.

"Christ almighty," I hissed, closing my eyes.

"I'd like you to fuck me good and hard, Reed," she crooned in my ear before licking it.

"Goddammit."

Someone honked behind us. I pulled over onto the shoulder and shoved my truck into park then somehow managed to disentangle her off my lap and put her back in the seat. I buckled the seatbelt so hard I was surprised I didn't bend the metal. Then I pointed a finger in her face.

"Stay in your fucking seat, Anna. Don't move till we get to the house."

She'd have to sleep in my bed, and I could take the

couch. My guest room had no bed and was more of a storage room for me and all my crap.

By the time I pulled into my drive, she was sullen and quiet. When I rounded the truck and pulled her back into my arms, she didn't try to put her arms around my neck, and it lacerated me. A silent tear streamed down her face.

"Anna, baby," I whispered into her hair as I carried her up my walkway and into my house. "It's okay. Please don't cry."

"Can't help it," she whispered then inhaled a sob, trying to keep quiet.

"I can't stand it if you cry, sweetheart." I carried her back to my bedroom.

"You're always saving me, Reed," she murmured against my neck, and I wanted to fall to the ground and swear to worship her for the rest of her life.

I set her on my bed and pulled back the covers, then slipped off her sandals and tucked her legs beneath them.

"Just like that first time…when you saved me from Blake Guidry."

My gaze shot to hers, but her eyes were closed and she was snuggling into the pillow.

"That was when I fell in love with you."

She was already still and asleep when my world was upended. When she said those words so softly, my pulse raced like mad, and a roar of triumph climbed up my throat, wanting to be thrown out into the world. Like those words hadn't just shattered me into a million pieces.

Like she hadn't just realigned my universe, the entire orbit shifting to circle wherever she went, wherever she was.

Hand trembling, I wiped the wet trail of tears from her cheek and pressed a kiss to the crown of her head. "Tomorrow, baby."

Tomorrow, I'd tell her what I wanted. I'd show her. Then I'd finally—fucking finally—I'd make her mine.

Chapter Eight

❧

~ANNA~

When I woke, the first thing I saw was a glass of water and two Advil sitting on the nightstand. But it wasn't my nightstand. Then I smelled *him* all around me. I was in Reed's bed.

Jerking upright—which wasn't smart after a night of heavy drinking—I quickly realized I was alone and still wearing my dress from last night.

"Oh, shit," I mumbled.

By some miracle, my headache was mild, but I felt exhausted. The alarm clock on the nightstand read 11:48. I'd slept nearly half the day. I took the Advil and drank down the water then pushed out of his bed and stared down at it. This wasn't how I'd hoped to end up in his bed.

Then I remembered trying to climb into his lap in his

truck while he was driving. I slapped both hands on my cheeks and squeezed my eyes shut, trying to forget what I'd said. "Oh, my God."

I tried to remember, skating through the fuzzy memories, recalling that I'd told him I wanted him to fuck me. "Oh. My. God."

I smelled something cooking but didn't hear him. Hurrying to the bathroom, I then shut the door and leaned over the sink, staring at myself in the mirror.

"This is a nightmare," I whispered to my horrific reflection, which looked like someone who'd had a bad trip and a long, wild night on the back of a motorcycle. Maybe with an entire motorcycle gang.

My hair was a rat's nest, sticking up everywhere. Mascara had smeared around my eyes, streaks of what must've been tears down one side of my face. "I cried?"

Jesus, Mary, and Joseph. How badly had I embarrassed myself?

I quickly locked the door, found a towel, and jumped in the shower. I needed to get myself looking more human and less hungover.

While showering, I tried not to think about the fact that this was where Reed got naked every night and scrubbed his body. But when I used his body wash, I whimpered at the scent I recognized on him so often. It wasn't exactly the same because this piney body wash was usually mixed with his own masculine smell. It was a mating call to my senses.

When I stepped out and toweled off, I remembered that he'd carried me inside. I thought I...

"No, you didn't."

Yes, I did. I'd said something about Blake Guidry and Reed being my hero. Then I quickly wiped those thoughts away. There was no way I'd be able to face him without being super embarrassed if I didn't turn off all thoughts of last night right this minute.

I pulled my bra back on then slipped my dress over my head, but I wasn't about to put on my panties from yesterday.

"Now what?" I looked around, trying to find a place to hide them.

Opening the cabinet below the sink, I balled them up and tucked them back behind some Drain-o. I could retrieve them Monday when I came to clean for him.

After using his brush to comb through my hair, I inspected myself in the mirror. My eyes were a little puffy, but I looked a hell of a lot better.

"Okay, you can do this," I mumbled to myself, inhaling a deep breath and leaving the bathroom to face him.

When I entered the kitchen, there was a platter of French fries on the counter. My stomach immediately growled. They looked a little crispy and some actually were burnt, but my empty, alcohol-lined stomach didn't care.

The backdoor swung open just then, and Reed walked in, carrying a tray of burgers. He stopped mid-step when he saw me, wearing those damn gray joggers, a tight white

T-shirt, and no shoes. Then he smiled, a great big swoony smile that nearly melted me onto the checkered tile of his kitchen.

"Hi," he said softly, still smiling. He carried the tray over to the counter and set it down right in front of me.

"Hi." I looked down, feeling the heat crawl up my neck and into my cheeks.

He placed both big hands on my bare upper arms and rubbed sensuously up and down. "How are you feeling?"

"Not so great. But not terrible."

"I figured." One of his hands drifted up to the side of my throat where he gave me a soft squeeze, his thumb brushing over my collar bone. I hitched in a breath, looking up at him in shock.

"You need a big burger and some greasy fries," he said softly before stepping away. "Best food to kill a hangover."

I nodded dumbly as he moved around the kitchen, pulling down plates.

"That sounds great. It smells delicious actually." My voice quivered a little. "I thought you couldn't cook."

He laughed as he pulled out mustard, mayonnaise, and ketchup from the fridge and set them on the counter. Then he grabbed a bottle of Tabasco Chipotle and set it out, too. A rumble of thunder rolled overhead.

"I can grill, but that's a far cry from cooking. I burnt the fries." A flash of lightning brightened the kitchen through the window over the sink. "Finished just in time, too."

Relieved that he was acting normal again and lightening the mood, I took a plate from him when he turned and offered. Maybe I hadn't embarrassed the hell out of myself after all.

"You first," he gestured.

Looking away, I made my burger. He waited for me to finish before he made his own.

"Why don't you go get *The Witcher* ready to go?" he suggested while he slathered mayo on two buns.

"Okay."

I walked zombie-like to his living room and turned on Netflix while settling onto my side of the sofa. A sweet sensation washed over me, loving that I had a *my side* of the sofa at Reed's house.

Another rumble of thunder vibrated the house. I glanced over my shoulder through the window over-looking the porch just as the first drops of rain began to fall. Then I settled back onto the couch, realizing it would be a while before we picked up my car downtown. And that was fine by me.

But also, what was happening here?

We'd fought at the Drunk Pelican before I stormed off. Then I ignored him all week, making sure I was gone before he got home every night. Then I got drunk and he picked me up. I said a bunch of crazy shit and attacked him in his truck and now he was being all sweet and acting like everything was normal. But also, not normal.

He was looking at me like...well, not the cautious or evasive way he did at my parents' house. It was more possessive and predatory and made my bones turn to liquid. Thank goodness, I was sitting down.

I started to eat and, immediately, the food made me feel better.

"Good?" he asked as he took his seat on the sofa, having balanced his plate on his forearm while he carried two glasses of iced tea for us to the coffee table.

"Mmhmm." I licked my lip and glanced up to find him staring at my mouth.

When I expected him to quickly look away like he usually did, he didn't. He did *not* look away. Rather, he remained still and focused, that wicked smile returning with a vengeance. Like he had every right to look at mouth like that.

What was happening right now?

I was nervous and excited and suddenly very horny.

"Finish eating," he ordered. "Then we'll watch the show."

Clearing my throat, I said, "Okay." Because what else was I supposed to do besides woodenly do what he said? Something was different.

We ate in silence, and I couldn't even look at him. But I sure as hell felt him staring at me. Strangely, it wasn't uncomfortable. It was thrilling and scary at the same time.

When I was finished, I wiped my hands on the napkin and drank the rest of my iced tea. When I started to get up to take his plate, he said, "I've got it."

I wasn't going to argue. He took our plates and glasses and returned to the kitchen. I settled back against the sofa. I grabbed the fleece throw folded on the end and spread it out over my lap.

When he returned, he paused, standing above the sofa, taking in my stance in the corner of the sofa.

"What?" I asked, that fluttery sensation returning ten-fold.

"Nah, we're not going to watch like that this afternoon."

"Huh?"

I was a brilliant conversationalist post-drinking.

He lifted the blanket and held out his hand. I put my hand in his and let him lift me out of my seat. Then he laid back down, stretching his body along the length of the sofa and pulled me down.

"Lay in front of me."

"What?" I blinked, confused.

"You heard me. Lay down in front of me, Anna."

"Um. Okay."

Again, brilliant verbiage coming out of my mouth because what the *hell* was going on?

I lay down, nervous and trying not to crowd him. But he only tucked me closer, his hand at my stomach pulling me back till he was perfectly spooning me. Then he flicked the fleece blanket over us with one hand.

"Comfortable?" he asked in a deep rumble close to my ear.

I couldn't refrain from shivering at the intimacy.

"Yes," I answered honestly, because what else was I supposed to do?

I was snuggled up on the sofa with Reed's giant body aligned behind every inch of mine, cocooned beneath a toasty blanket and toasty man. His arm was wrapped around my waist, keeping me pressed against him, his fingers curling beneath my opposite hip pressed into the sofa.

"Get the remote and turn it on," he murmured. "I'm not moving. This is perfect."

Pulse racing wildly, I reached out and picked up the remote then turned on *The Witcher*. But my mind—for once—was not on Henry Cavill while watching it. It was one-hundred percent on the delicious man glued to my body from behind.

My head resting on his bicep, my hands folded under my chin, my vagina wondered how we'd passed out last night and woken up in heaven.

I tried to focus on the show, but it was simply impossible. And that was before he nuzzled my wet hair to the side and started kissing the underside of my jaw. Gasping, I didn't move, hoping this wasn't a dream. I'd had fantasies of something like this happening.

He trailed soft, warm kisses up to my ear then down my throat, my heart racing.

"Reed?" I whispered.

"Hmm?" He nipped the skin at the base of my throat.

"What's happening right now?"

He licked a trail up my throat then lifted his head, his mouth inches from mine. His piercing gaze was hungry and dark, his voice a husky rasp.

"Anna."

"Huh?"

He cupped one side of my face, his hand gentle but his voice rough and harsh when he said, "I've waited for years for this. I've fantasized about taking you so many times and in so many ways, you should probably be afraid."

"I'm not afraid." My chest was rising and falling quickly, but it wasn't fear that had my heartrate spiking.

"Tell me now if this is what you want," he demanded, "because I'm not letting you go once we do this. Your brothers will have to beat me till I'm dead, Anna, and I'm not joking."

There was a primal gleam in his eyes that should've put me off, made me push back. I realized then I was seeing the secret side of Reed he held in check and hidden from the rest of the world—an obsessive, possessive side focused entirely on me. All I wanted was to have all of him, take all of him.

"This is what I want," I finally confessed, then I reached up and combed my fingers into the back of his hair.

A flicker of heat skated over his expression before he slanted his mouth over mine and groaned into my mouth. His tongue stroked deep, and I whimpered beneath his invasion. Because that's exactly what it felt like when his hand at my hip roamed to mound my breast and squeeze, his leg slid between my thighs, and he kissed the breath out of me.

I gasped when he broke the kiss and then arched my

neck as he made his way down my throat with teeth and tongue and mind-hazing kisses.

"So fucking sweet," he murmured against the top curve of my breast before he slid the strap off my shoulder, trailing his tongue along the top edge of my bra.

Then he shot up onto his knees, staring down with feral fixation. I pushed the hem of his T-shirt up, showing him what I wanted. He didn't hesitate but reached back and pulled it off in seconds.

He lowered both my dress straps and eased them down, bunching the dress at my waist. I lifted onto my elbows and managed to unhook my bra, then slid it off both shoulders and tossed it to the floor as I eased back down.

His eyes glittered in the darkness of the room, the storm blowing and pounding hard outside. He picked up the remote and turned the television off, removing all sound but the thunderstorm crashing down around us.

Reed lowered again, planting one hand by my shoulder on the sofa, one leg still between my thighs. He coasted light fingertips over one breast and then the other, flicking his thumb over each nipple then pinching lightly on the right peak.

"Unh," was all I managed to say, one hand gripping the edge of the sofa, the other wrapped around his forearm.

He kept his torso above me as he explored, his free hand roaming along the side of my ribcage then over my stomach, skimming the bunched fabric of my dress to the hem at my thigh. That's when his heated gaze returned to mine.

He watched me as he parted my thighs, trailing lightly up my inner thigh. He slid his two fingers up my slit and arched a brow. "No panties." His gaze darkened with a wicked gleam, and his mouth ticked up on one side. "So wet, Anna."

I clawed into his muscular forearm; my only other response was my hips lifting toward his questing fingers. He strummed my clit with his thumb, and then with his jaw clenched, eyes fierce, he slid two fingers inside me.

His arm collapsed, then he lowered himself onto his elbow as he closed his eyes and pressed his forehead to mine.

"Yes," I whispered, gripping his shoulders and rocking up, riding his fingers.

"Goddamn, Anna," he ground out. "I'm trying to regain control here so I don't fuck you too hard."

"You can fuck me hard, Reed. You can fuck me however you want." When I fisted the back of his hair, his eyes went flinty.

He pulled his hand free and licked his fingers clean. I whimpered at the sight. Then he flipped up the skirt of my dress and stared down, making a primitive sound in his throat as he lifted me under my arms and shoved me up till my shoulders were propped on the sofa arm. Easing onto the floor, he shifted my body diagonally, his hands cupping my ass. He lifted my hips and opened his hot mouth on my pussy.

"Ah!" I cried out, digging my heels into his back.

"So fucking good," he murmured against me before flicking with his tongue then sucking on my clit.

"Reed!" I screamed, my climax spiraling too fast like the storm outside.

My thighs quivered as I arched my spine and moaned, coming in his mouth. He held me tight, not relenting, sucking and licking and groaning like I was the best feast he'd ever had. When my clit became too sensitive, I pulled at his hair, trying to get away but also still needing him wildly.

"Reed," I begged, though I wasn't exactly sure for what.

He leveraged up onto his knees and gripped the cloth of my dress, still bunched around my waist and pulled it down and off my legs, tossing it aside.

"What—?"

Before I could finish my question, he'd picked me up and flipped me on my knees so that I faced the back of the sofa. He placed a palm at the center of my back and eased my torso forward so that I leaned on the sofa back.

"Open your knees wider," he ordered gruffly.

I did and then looked over my shoulder when I heard him stand up. He pushed his joggers and briefs off. My gaze dropped to his phenomenally well-made and rather large dick, standing straight up against his lower abdomen.

"You like what you see?"

My gaze shot to his as he stroked himself leisurely. But there was nothing calm or leisurely about the look in his eyes. My pussy squeezed at the sight of him, the wetness between my thighs increasing.

"Very much," I finally answered. His gaze was on my ass. I could only imagine how I looked, partially bent on the sofa, open and ready for him. "You like what *you* see?"

Then he was moving, settling his knees right on the inside of mine, widening my stance. "You have no fucking idea," he rumbled into my ear as he lined up his dick at my entrance.

He wrapped a hand around the front of my throat, holding me firmly but gently. He eased in, inch by inch, stretching me till it felt so tight.

"Arch your back. Take me, baby." He bit my nape.

I arched more, moaning as he sank in deeper, the delicious feel of him hazing my senses.

"Yes...more."

Then he was in to the hilt, his pelvis flush against my ass. "That's my girl." He ground in a circle while my body stretched for him.

"Hold onto the sofa back. It's going to be rough."

I gripped the cushioned edges as his palm at my throat slid down between my thighs, the calloused pad of one finger circling my clit. He gripped my hip hard with the other and started to fuck me.

"Oh, God," I murmured, head dropping. I pressed my cheek into the cushion.

An animalistic growl rumbled from Reed as he pounded in and out, flesh slapping faster and faster.

"Fuck, fuck, fuck," he cursed, his fingers digging into

my hip, his thumb flicking my clit faster. "You're so tight and sweet. I'm going to come too soon."

The sound of him losing control shot me over the edge again. I screamed and bit the sofa cushion as my inner walls clamped and rippled around him.

"*Christ*, Anna," he grumbled, pressing our bodies into the sofa back, trapping his hand against my pussy.

He cupped me there, sliding two fingers into the slickness of my folds as he made jerky, short thrusts inside me till he held deep on a long, feral groan.

"Just like that," he whispered in my ear. "You're going to kill me, Anna." He dropped his forehead to my neck, breathing hard, his dick still pulsing inside me.

I would've laughed if I didn't feel like crying. Not sad crying, just an overwhelming release of emotions.

"Oh, shit." He tensed, still holding me intimately.

"What?" I heard the panic in my voice.

"I forgot to use a condom."

I laughed at that, a tear slipping free as well. "I thought you suddenly regretted it."

He pulled out of me and sat on the sofa, hauling me onto his lap. It was the most awkward but also sweet thing to be cradled naked in his arms like this. He nudged my chin up till my gaze met his.

"I'd never regret this. Or you." He shook his head adamantly. "Not ever." He wiped the one lone tear away with his thumb. "You okay?"

"Better than I've ever been," I admitted. "And I'm on the pill. We're safe."

He cradled me closer, and I wrapped my arms around his neck, my body pressed into his wide, warm chest.

"Anna, I'm not going anywhere. If you got pregnant, that would just speed up our timeline." He paused then added hesitantly. "If that's what you wanted."

My stomach dropped. "Our timeline?"

He brushed his lips against mine. "I'm all in, pretty girl." Another light sweep of warm lips. "Unless you kick me to the curb. And even then, you'll have a hard time getting rid of me."

I pressed a soft kiss to his mouth. "I don't want to get rid of you. I want you to stay." I gulped against the fear I was feeling.

Rather than being shocked, he simply smiled, pressed one more quick kiss to my lips, and stood with me still in his arms. "Let's go to my bedroom. I'm not done with you yet."

"I can't believe this turn of events from last week, but I'm not going to argue since you somehow got some sense knocked into you."

"You knocked some sense into me." He grinned down at me as he carried me down the hallway.

"Me?"

"You told me last night you were in love with me."

"What?!" I did *not* remember that. "I didn't."

"You did." He grinned wider as he tossed me on the bed then crushed his body on top of mine. "And don't try to take it back. You also told me that you tended to speak more honestly when you were drunk."

"I'm not trying to take it back," I said to his chin, suddenly shy and unsure.

"Hey." He lifted my chin again to look at him. "I love you, Anna. *So* much."

Then he kissed me like he hadn't just rocked my whole world. It started light and sweet, but when I teased my tongue inside his mouth, the kiss turned hotter. I opened my legs till he was cradled between and where he was growing hard against my hip.

When he lifted up and looked over at his nightstand, I gripped his shoulders and hauled him back down. "Don't worry about the condoms."

I reached between us and gripped his hard dick. He hissed in a breath, pumping into my hand. Then I lined him up, and he rocked into me. We sank together on a mutual, deep groan.

"You're definitely trying to kill me." He hooked his arm under one of my knees and spread me wide, stroking in slow and deep. "I'm never going to be able to keep my hands off of you now."

"Who said you have to?"

When I saw his brow purse into a frown, no doubt thinking of Jonah, I clawed my nails down his back, bringing his focus back to me. "Give me more, Reed."

So he did, angling in a way that dragged over my clit just right. I tilted my head back and let go, let the man I loved bring us both to complete and total bliss. We could worry about all the secrets tomorrow.

Chapter Nine

❦

~REED~

I REALIZED I WAS UNCHARACTERISTICALLY SMILING TO
myself as I jogged across Main Street toward Anna's
studio. Her car was in the lot, so I knew she was already
here. I'd texted her thirty minutes ago to meet me because
I had a surprise.

After I'd confessed to Hale that Anna and I were, in
fact, dating, even though we had no immediate plans to
tell her family, Hale had decided to help me gain some
boyfriend points by finishing her studio in record time.

We'd finished putting up the final mirrors and the
dance bar along the wall by lunchtime today. I owed Hale
big time. And who knew he was such a romantic?

When I opened the door, I heard music playing.
Locking the door behind me out of habit, I peeked

around the corner of the foyer entrance to find her dancing.

My heart squeezed, and my stomach knotted. I hadn't seen her dance since her final recital as a senior in high school when the whole family, including me, was forced to attend. While Jonah had grumbled at the ridiculous unfairness of being forced to sit through a three-hour recital, I'd silently basked in the joy of watching her perform each routine that night.

Right now, she moved fluidly to what I knew was a lyrical type of dance—because I'd taken the time to learn each genre she performed. Florence and the Machine crooned a sorrowful tune while she leaped and turned and arched with magnificent grace in her cut-offs, tank top, and bare feet.

She stopped suddenly when she caught sight of me in the mirror, her chest heaving.

"You're so beautiful," I admitted, elated that I finally could.

I walked slowly across the room. She went toward the mirror and tapped the music off on her phone, which was sitting on the floor. She stood and smiled, watching my reflection as I drew closer and then wrapped my arms around her.

"Do you like it?" I asked her.

"It's unbelievable, Reed. I can't believe you finished so quickly."

"You want to get those summer camps organized, right? Hale helped me knock it out pretty fast for you."

"I don't know how to thank you." She had her arms over mine and squeezed them tighter to her.

"You don't have to thank me." I pressed my lips to her neck and inhaled the sweetest fragrance on the planet. Pure Anna.

Suddenly, she pushed out of my arms, turned, and lowered to her knees. My body locked tight automatically.

"Anna, you don't have to do that."

A playful sparkle was in her eyes as her hands went to my belt. "I've been wanting to do this to you since I first discovered what a blow job was."

My body was rigid and wanting, but I kept still, only letting my hand drift to her jaw to feel the softness of her silken skin.

"When was that?"

"When I was fourteen and Emma showed me a porn video on her brand-new cell phone." She had my belt buckle undone and was working on my button and zipper. "I couldn't believe her mom didn't block it, but she told me it was her mom who showed her the site so she could learn more about sex."

I started to laugh, but then she reached into my jeans under my boxers and wrapped her hand around my dick. I hissed in a breath and slid my fingers into her hair, which was down today. She smiled up at me as she pulled my jeans lower around my hips and slid her mouth open slowly around the crown.

"Fucking hell." I fisted her hair but didn't force her

forward like I wanted. I let her take the lead. "So you've been fantasizing about sucking my cock?"

She let the tip pop free and then swiped her tongue in a circle. Complete torture.

"For years," she whispered before swallowing me halfway down.

"Unh. Fuck." I had both hands in her hair now, one sliding to her nape so I could gently tug her forward. "Deeper. You can take more. I know you can."

Her eyes watered, but she opened wider and let me hit the back of her throat. She moaned and sucked hard at the head before plunging forward again. I refused to think about how she'd perfected that technique, because no one's dick would ever be in her mouth but mine from here on out.

I let go of her hair and cradled her jaw, my palm flush and my thumb sliding along her lower lip to feel where she was sucking me inside her.

Then she started bobbing faster, and my thighs locked tight. That fiery sensation was barreling closer, lightning fast.

"I'm going to come, baby." I pressed back a little, getting ready, but her hands at my hips shot around to my ass, holding me hard as she took me deeper.

"You wanna swallow me?"

She grunted with a jerky nod.

"Fuck, you look so beautiful sucking me deep."

She smiled around my cock. She knew.

"Anna, sweetheart," I whispered, unable to say another thing.

I clenched her neck tight but let my head fall back as I pumped a little deeper and came down her throat. A sizzle of fire electrified my thighs and up my spine, tightening my balls to near pain. I'd never come like that in my life.

A noise jarred me loose from my orgasmic ecstasy. Someone was trying to open the door. I jerked out of her mouth and started zipping and buckling.

"You expecting someone?" I asked.

"No." She was wiping her mouth with the back of her hand, panting, her lips puffy and swollen from sucking my dick. If we hadn't been interrupted, I was going to return the favor.

"Why don't you go to the office?" I suggested.

"Why? They probably want to see me anyway. It could be the plumber to redo the bathroom, though our appointment was next week."

My instincts were telling me differently, especially when Hale kept telling me I needed to stop keeping secrets. "Just go to your office till we know who it is."

She slipped off into the small office area and shut the door till it was barely cracked.

I marched across the studio and into the small entrance and opened the door, my stomach dropping out. "Hi, Jonah."

Scowling, he pushed past me and stormed into the room. Hands on his hips, he spun around slowly, taking in my toolkit still sitting against the wall with the dance bar.

His face was flushed red. I knew the signs of Jonah's anger. I also knew how to deal with him, so I kept quiet and waited, thankful that Anna stayed hidden.

"Where's my sister?" he spat out, glaring at me now.

"Not here right now."

He looked at the wall of mirrors and shook his head. "I can't fucking believe you two, going behind my back."

My heart triple-paced, and something twisted in my stomach.

"My parents' too," he continued. "They were against this studio thing, but you helped her do it anyway. I can't fucking believe you!"

I experienced a split-second moment of relief that he wasn't talking about us dating, but about the studio, then a bolt of anger shot up my spine. "She's a grown woman. She can decide what she wants to do with her life."

"Even if she's throwing all her life savings away on this dream that could crash and burn and blow up in her face, leaving her with nothing?" He was borderline yelling, but I kept cool.

Crossing my arms, I held his gaze. "If she crashes and burns, there will be people there to pick her back up. She won't have *nothing*. And this is a fine speech coming from someone who has no job and is spending his days writing the all-American novel."

He glared, and I glared back. Finally, he blew out a breath. "It's not the all-American novel. It's way cooler than that."

I didn't respond. He'd insulted Anna, and I was having a hard time reeling in my rage.

"You always did have a soft spot for her." He glanced around and nodded. "At least you and Hale did a bang-up job on the place. Looks awesome."

Just like that, Jonah was calm again. His mood swings were notorious. He could lose his shit in a heartbeat, then be right as rain two minutes later. That's why I always waited him out.

"Believe it or not, we are really fucking good at our jobs."

He chuckled. "Yeah, yeah. But you're going to have to tell my parents this Sunday. I'm not keeping this kind of fucking secret from them."

"Fine. I'll relay that to Anna."

He nodded. "Good. I can't wait to see you get your ass handed to you by my dad."

I rolled my eyes. His dad loved me, but I was hoping he wouldn't hate me for this. Still, I was behind Anna one-hundred percent no matter what.

"You all finished?" Jonah pointed to my toolkit all tucked away. "Hale was going to meet us at the Drunk Pelican."

"That's how you knew where I was?"

"Yeah. Hale's a shit-stirrer. He told me to check out the new dance studio on Main Street to find you."

Fucking Hale.

"I need to do a few more things then call it a night. It

was a long day." And I just wanted to curl into bed with Anna.

"You sure? I've got some fine girls I met at Starbucks coming to meet us. You need to get laid, man."

For a second, I couldn't even respond. Then finally, I shook my head. "I'm good."

"Seriously? You've been abstinent for like a year or something, right? These girls are ready to go, I'm telling you."

"Not interested, Jonah. And why the hell were you at Starbucks?"

"Needed a nice environment to write. They've got cool vibes there."

"You're actually turning into a cliché. Since when did you become a hipster?"

"Fuck off, dude." He marched for the door. "If you change your mind, there's a pretty blonde waiting at the Drunk Pelican for you." Then he grinned and walked out the door.

I locked it behind him, relieved that my safety precautions always had me doing that. I'm not sure how much blood would've been on these floors had Jonah walked in on me with Anna on her knees and my dick in her mouth a few minutes ago.

A pretty blonde waiting for me. Like I cared. There was also a pretty blonde now storming out of her office with her purse on her shoulder. She marched straight to the mirror and bent to pick up her phone where she'd left it. She was fuming.

"Hey, hey." I grabbed her by the shoulders to face me. "Look, we'll tell your parents together. It'll be fine."

"I don't care about that. I'm mad that my stupid brother is trying to set you up with some blond bimbo barista."

I laughed, which wasn't the smart thing to do. She wiggled to get free, but I held her tighter, pulling her into my chest. She kept her arms at her sides and looked away.

"I have no intentions of taking your brother up on his offer. I have exactly what I want right here in my arms."

"He's an asshat."

"Yeah." I nuzzled into her hair and kissed her neck. "He is."

She huffed and let out a breath. "I don't want to keep secrets anymore."

"I know." I pulled back to look at her. "We're going to tell your parents about the studio on Sunday."

"No." She staked me with those sweet brown eyes that could make me do anything. "We're telling them about us."

I stiffened, mulling that over. I didn't want to keep us a secret either, but I also didn't want to overwhelm them with two giant blows at one time. And I wanted to live in our peaceful bubble a little longer before I had to deal with the possibility my best friend might hate me after this.

"Are you embarrassed to be with me?" She tilted her head defiantly.

"Hell no. Of course not."

"Then we're telling them."

"Fine."

She wiggled loose, her temper still spiking. "I'm going to go."

"No, you're not." I plucked her purse off her shoulder and tossed it aside.

She caught the look in my eyes and started backing up. "I'm not in the mood."

"Why?" I continued to corral her back toward the mirror. "Because Jonah made you jealous of some girl I have no intention of hooking up with?"

Her chin tilted up, her expression mutinous. But then she said, "Yes."

"Then you're not leaving till I prove to you who I belong to."

Her back was against the mirror now. "I don't want to play."

"Yes you do. What you don't want is to think about me with another woman." I stood inches from her and worked on her button and zipper. She didn't resist me. "And you still think there's some chance in hell that I'd take another woman to bed when I have you. So we're going to get some things straight right here and now." I jerked her shorts and panties down as I fell to my knees. "I don't want you to ever wonder about me. This is the only pussy I ever want."

Then I spread her open with my thumb and forefinger and sucked her clit into my mouth. Her knees buckled on a whimpered cry, both her hands clutching at my hair.

"Reed," she cried out.

I licked and sucked her into oblivion, spreading her slickness with two fingers before pushing inside her. Her hands in my hair curled into claws against my scalp, but I didn't let up. Not for a second.

When her breaths became shallower and her moans louder, I unbuckled my belt and unzipped my jeans. When she cried out, rippling around my fingers, I rocketed to my feet, twisted her to face the mirror, and plunged inside her.

Her hands were splayed on the mirror, her eyes wide, watching me as I fucked her so hard she came up onto her toes. She could barely spread her legs with her shorts at her knees, but the tight sweetness of her ass and thighs made the sensation more erotic.

I slid one hand beneath her tank and pushed her bra up so I could mound her breast, my other was between her legs, working her clit. She squirmed, so sensitive from her orgasm still milking my dick, but I gave her no room to come down or to get away.

Holding her gaze in the reflection, I rumbled softly against her ear. "This sweet, sweet pussy owns me."

She let her head fall to my shoulder, her darkened gaze, intent on me in the mirror.

"This dick is only going inside one woman from here on out. You hear me?" I ground deeper, harder, clutching her to me and holding her practically off the ground as I sank deeper with each stroke. "Tell me who owns my body. And this cock inside you."

"I do." Her hands left the mirror, curled around my

wrists and squeezed, holding me to her, not pushing away. "I own them."

"That's right, my angel. *You* do." I pinched her nipple, and she whimpered. "Now squeeze my cock and make me come inside you."

She did, her heated gaze so sensual and sexy I couldn't hold back any longer. My mouth opened, and I grunted with two more sharp thrusts then held deep and hard. The fact that my sweet Anna, pretty pink princess her whole life, took my dirty mouth and hard cock so good nearly undid me altogether. She liked the dirty side of me. I'd even say she loved it. And it made me want her more, love her more.

"I love you," she whispered to my reflection, her voice shaky.

"I love you, too, Anna." I kissed her jaw, holding her gaze in the mirror. "Giving my body to someone else would be breaking my own heart. So you never have to wonder or worry about that."

She nodded, a tear slipping down her soft cheek. I pulled out and turned her. When I kissed her sweet mouth, she practically devoured me, her arms tight around my neck. I wrapped an arm around her waist, one hand on her ass as I kissed her hard.

When we finally broke apart, she murmured against my mouth, "Let's go home and take a shower together."

Again, my heart squeezed because she called my house *home*. Exactly where I wanted her. Always.

"Sounds like a good plan." I popped her on the ass, and she squealed. I let her wiggle away.

After we both had our pants back on, she gasped. "Oh, no. I was so excited to get here that I forgot to cook dinner."

"We can get take-out. I'm in the mood for a fried oyster po'boy."

"Mmm, yeah. That sounds great," she said as we walked to the door hand-in-hand. "I'm going to make you my lasagna tomorrow night though."

"You don't have to cook and clean for me anymore. The job is done."

"Now, I want to," she said with that shy tilt of her head, looking away.

Stopping her at the door, I pulled her back into my arms before we headed outside. "How about this? You cook, and I'll clean the dishes. We'll split laundry and cleaning the house. Though you might hate me if I ruin your cute dresses in the wash."

Her brown eyes widened. "My dresses?"

It was my turn to feel shy. Maybe this was too soon, but I couldn't help myself. "You're it for me, Anna. I'd like you to move in...if you want."

A huge smile broke across her face as she launched up and hugged me tight. "I'd love to. When?"

"How about Sunday night? After we tell your family."

"Yeah," she laughed, "we might both want to be scarce after that."

So she wouldn't get a sense of the dread I had for

Sunday, I grabbed her hand and led her out and across Main Street toward the plaza parking lot. Anna would never lose her family, but I could certainly lose my best friend. And the only family I'd ever known.

I'd risk it for Anna. I'd risk everything for her. But it didn't make the heartache or fear disappear.

Chapter Ten

✦✦✦

~ANNA~

AT THE SOUND OF SOMEONE COMING IN THE BACKDOOR, MY stomach did a triple-flip. Reed always came in the backdoor without knocking. I was in the kitchen, tossing a green salad while Mom stirred the sausage and tasso jambalaya that had just finished cooking.

"Just in time, sweetheart," she said lightly to the fine as hell man who made my knees buckle as he entered the kitchen, a small ice chest in hand.

"Smells delicious, Ms. Dinah."

"Hope you brought your appetite because there's plenty."

"Oh, I did." But his gaze was on me, not my Mom's jambalaya.

I'd worn a pretty floral summer dress with a delicate

ruffle at the hem which hit right above my knees. It tied in a halter-top style behind my neck. I knew this one made my boobs look great, and I wanted to look my best for him.

Still, I was utterly shocked how openly he was eating me up with his fire-blue eyes. I could already hear the naughty words he'd say to me later as he slipped his hand up my skirt. I squeezed my thighs together at the hungry look of his and mouthed *stop it*.

To which, he simply grinned and said, "Jonah and Mr. Jimmy outside?"

"Yeah. They're waiting on your drinks."

His gaze lingered on me long enough to make my cheeks go hot, then I turned away to finish the salad.

"Bring it to the table when it's ready, sweetheart," Mom said, carrying the Magnalite pot of jambalaya.

Deep breath in and out, I followed her a minute later. The basket of bread rolls was already there.

"Justin, honey, grab the butter out of the fridge," she told my brother as he came in the sliding door.

"Sure thing, Mom."

Then Dad, Jonah, and Reed followed, laughing about something, carrying their Old Fashioneds that Reed had provided again. Jessie came in right after, tapping away on his phone.

"Y'all get seated and pass your plates," Mom said.

Mom liked to serve from the table, but she also liked to be the one dishing out the main course. Everyone took a seat, Reed right next to me as he usually was. Funny, I'd never noticed that his permanent place here at our table had always been right beside me. Like he belonged at my side. That gave me a little courage for what was about to come.

"Smells great, Mom," said Jonah, shoving his plate in front of Reed's to get served first.

"Your dad's request since we hadn't had it in a while."

The typical Sunday dinner chaos commenced, plates clinking and being passed, hands reaching for the salad bowl and breadbasket. Mom fetched her pitcher of iced tea and set it on the table then settled in her chair and we all dove in.

"So how's work, Reed?" Dad asked.

"Very good, sir. Lots of work. Can't complain."

"That's right, son. Keeps the paychecks coming."

Jonah reached for a second roll. "Yeah, what other special projects have you been working on, *Reed*?"

My limbs locked up, and I set my fork down. Jonah had asked it so suggestively that, of course, my Dad quirked a frown in his direction.

"Got something special on the line?" Dad asked, taking another bite of jambalaya.

Reed cleared his throat, his gaze sliding to me, then he fiddled with his napkin in his lap. "Actually, I did just finish a project I'd like to tell you about."

"No, Reed," I interrupted, "I'll tell them."

My Dad's frown deepened, and my Mom's gaze popped up from her salad. Neither said a word, and my brothers were suddenly no longer eating. Except for

Justin. He just kept shoveling even though I was obviously about to make a huge announcement.

"I bought the old Romero insurance office on Main Street. And I traded cooking and cleaning with Reed for his help in renovating it into my studio. It's finished, and it's beautiful. I'm opening for summer classes next month."

I spit it out fast so no one could say anything otherwise. I felt like I was going to vomit while waiting for Dad to unfreeze and say something.

His frown slid to Reed. "You did this, Reed? When you knew we didn't want her taking a risk on this business so soon?"

There was no doubt my father was fuming, his face flushed with anger. My mom patted his arm.

"Yes, sir," said Reed without flinching a muscle, holding Dad's frowning gaze.

"I thought you'd respect me more than that."

"It wasn't that I didn't respect you, Mr. Jimmy. It's that I respected Anna's wishes more."

Those intense blue eyes swiveled to me, and there was no doubt he had feelings for me by the way he looked at me. I couldn't breathe as I stared back at him.

"I'd do anything for Anna," he said, the entire room deadly silent. Even Justin. "She's smart and capable and she knows what she's doing. I believe in her, even if y'all don't." He took my hand that was resting on the table and laced our fingers together, smiling so wide I couldn't help but love him even more. "Whatever Anna wants, I'm going to support her." Then he turned his gaze to my parents. "Because I love her."

That's when I finally decided to be brave enough to look at the shocked and blank faces of my parents and brothers. Surprisingly, it was Jessie who broke the vacuum-like silence first.

"I told you." He nudged Jonah next to him. "You owe me a hundred bucks."

Reed and I both turned to Jonah, who made a disgusted face.

"Fucking hell, Reed. You lost me a hundred bucks!"

"Language, Jonah," Mom warned before hopping up out of her chair and running to Reed's chair to hug him from behind. She squished her cheek to his. "I'm so happy to finally hear this, sweetheart."

Dad's frown had morphed into a tilted smile. He sighed. "I'm not happy about this studio business yet, but I'm happy as hell to hear you finally wised up about Anna."

"Still makes me a little sick," said Justin, shoving food in his mouth.

My pulse pounded in my throat as I tried to absorb what they were saying. "Wait a minute!" All eyes came to me. "You mean to tell me that you've always thought Reed and I had a thing for each other?"

Jessie scoffed. "Like it wasn't obvious."

Reed tilted his head back and laughed so hard I couldn't help but join him. Then he turned and kissed my cheek. "Guess we had nothing to worry about after all."

I leaned forward to whisper in his ear, "Not until we

tell them I'm moving in with you."

"Disgusting! Not at the table," yelled Jonah, lobbing a napkin across the table.

"Jonah, don't throw things at the table, dear," Mom fussed. "Now, let's all finish our meal while it's hot. After dinner, Anna can tell us about her new studio."

Leave it to Mom to smooth things over like all was right with the world. When I glanced at Reed next to me, smiling, I honestly felt that it was.

After dinner, Reed was helping me clean the dishes in the kitchen when Jonah strolled in and planted himself next to the sink.

"My sister? Gross, man."

"There is *nothing* gross about your sister."

"Shut the fuck up." He put his hands over his ears. "I can't hear that shit without wanting to vomit."

"Good, then leave. We were about to start making out."

Jonah looked horrified and hurried from the room. I belted out a laugh right before Reed pulled me into his arms and buried his face against my neck, laughing.

"I don't know what we were so worried about," he whispered against my temple.

I shook my head. "They all knew?"

"Crazy." He pulled back to look down at me. "Guess I haven't been so secretive about my feelings all these years after all."

"All these...*years*?"

He'd felt this way about me for years? My whole body soared and melted against him.

"There's a reason I never brought a girl home," he whispered against my jaw, hugging me tighter. "The girl I wanted was here all along."

"Oh, Reed."

Then we were kissing, my hands curling into his hair. When he slanted his mouth to go deeper, I heard someone step into the room.

"Gross!" Justin turned back around. "*Mom*, make Reed and Anna stop kissing in the kitchen. My whole dinner is going to come back up."

"Leave them alone," I heard her say while Reed and I started laughing again.

One of his hands slid down my back and down to the hem of my skirt where he coasted his fingertips over the back of my bare thigh, raising goosebumps on my skin.

"I like this dress." His voice had gone deep and rough as he continued to trail along my lower thigh, back and forth.

"I wore it for you."

"We'd better let them know our third bit of news then so I can take you home and you can take it off for me."

"Why don't we just sneak out instead? I'm afraid my brothers may actually rupture their guts and die at the thought of me moving into your house with you."

"Sounds good to me."

I glanced through the archway into the living room where everyone was settled in and watching Deadliest Catch, then I grabbed my purse, took Reed's hand, and tip-toed toward the door leading to the garage.

We hurried to his truck and took off like two sneaky kids, laughing the whole way back to his house. Funny thing was, even after he'd taken me against the kitchen wall, still in my dress, then again in the shower before we collapsed on the sofa, snuggling naked under the covers, not one person had texted us.

It was around midnight after we'd finished the second episode of *The Witcher* when Reed's phone lit up with a text. Jonah.

He reached over me to the coffee table and held it up where we could both read it.

JONAH: You've always been my brother. Guess it'll be official.

I choked. We'd just started dating! No one said anything about marriage yet. Jeesh. Then another text.

JONAH: Because if you don't marry her now, I'll fucking kill you.

Reed laughed, his chest shaking behind me. He started texting back over my head where I could see exactly what he typed.

REED: We'll be brothers in truth soon enough. Whenever Anna says yes.

Then he set the phone aside and cuddled me close again. Adrenaline had shot through me at his casual response about marrying me.

"You have to ask me first."

He pressed a kiss right under my jaw. "I will."

Then we went back to watching TV till we fell asleep together on our sofa.

Epilogue

❧

~REED~

"A huge thank you goes to my boyfriend, Reed Robicheaux, and Hale Broussard with Hale Building Company for making the renovations. And again, thank you to Beauville Chamber of Commerce for your support."

Anna stood in a pale blue dress and dark denim jacket in front of the red ribbon beneath the new sign, *Dream On Studios*. She was talking softly to the representative from the Chamber of Commerce. With a nudge from Hale, whose father was a friend of the representative, they'd set Anna's grand opening—noting that her building was in the historic district of Beauville—with a ribbon cutting and publicity. Everyone applauded and glanced toward me and Hale standing off to the side as she took the scissors and cut the ribbon.

A loud roar of cheers and applause went up with the sudden sound of Bruno Mars filling the blocked-off area in front of the dance studio. Her summer camp students—now her fall semester students—all dressed in matching black and pink polka-dotted leotards, started a high-energy routine they'd learned at camp.

The crowd cheered as they performed with near-perfect accuracy, zipping and hip-hopping, or whatever it is they called it. All I knew was they looked amazing, and there were smiles on every parent who came out for the cutting and the performance.

My girlfriend's face was beaming, and I couldn't imagine life getting any better than this. Actually, I could. It was too soon, but I was hoping by Christmas I could call Anna my fiancé.

"Nice job, son," said Mr. Jimmy next to me, clapping a hand on my shoulder. "I know I had my doubts, and honestly, I still do, but…seeing Anna's face lit up like that and so happy, I guess I need to just hope she knows what she's doing."

"Yes, sir." I wasn't about to tell the man who'd been a father to me my whole life that he had been wrong in ever doubting her.

He chuckled. "What you really mean is, 'Shove it, old man. Anna will succeed no matter what she does.'"

I laughed then. "Not exactly, but I do think she knows

what she's doing. And if she doesn't, I'll be here to catch her."

"You'll see one day. When you and Anna have a daughter of your own."

A spike of shock hit me as I turned to him. I'd never told anyone but Jonah that I hoped and intended to marry her.

Mr. Jimmy smiled. "Come on now, son. You've been in love with my daughter for years now. And better yet, you two suit each other. She'll keep you from being too quiet and isolated and you'll keep her grounded and focused. It'll be a good life together."

A lump lodged in my throat as I said, "I'd hoped to ask you for her hand around Thanksgiving. Didn't want to ask her too soon."

"Nah." He clapped my shoulder and then dropped his hand. "She's been waiting for you since...I'd say that time you picked her up when she fell off the trampoline." He shook his head. "I went to help her, but she went to you instead of me that day. I knew then you'd likely end up together. Jonah might've brought you home, but it was Anna who kept you there."

Then he walked off toward Ms. Dinah, talking to a dancer's parent in passing as if he hadn't just shocked the hell out of me.

"Okay, man." Jonah popped up beside me, Hale moving closer. "Let's head to the Drunk Pelican after this. They've got two-for-one margaritas, and nothing draws the ladies like a margarita happy hour."

"I'm down," said Hale. "That bartender is hot as fuck."

"I'll check with Anna."

"Damn, you're so pussy-whipped."

"Yeah," I agreed. "And a mighty fine p—"

Jonah clamped a hand over my mouth. "Don't you even fucking say it. I might've agreed to all this shit, but you will not talk about my sister's...body parts."

Laughing, I shoved him off. "Fine. We'll have to ask Emma, too." She was chatting up Anna as they watched the dancers pop a final pose in their routine.

The cheers escalated again, then everyone was milling around. The girls, and even a few male dancers, ran up to Anna excitedly for her approval. She shot me a smile across the lot that hit me right in the heart.

"Yeah, Emma can come," agreed Jonah, hissing in a breath and checking Emma out. "She's looking fine this afternoon."

"You don't stand a chance," I told him. "She's not your type."

"Maybe so. But that girl can dance."

Right then, Anna and Emma sidled over.

"Your ears were burning?" Jonah asked Emma.

"What were you saying?"

"That you could dance, and I expect one when we go to the Drunk Pelican tonight."

"It's Thursday, dipwit." She flicked him in the ear.

"Ow!"

"No dancing tonight." Then Emma's eyes lit up excitedly as she rubbed her hands together. "It's trivia night, and I'm kickass at trivia."

"I thought it was margarita night," I aimed at Jonah.

"It is," offered Emma. "They like to get us good and sauced before trivia. It makes the competition a little rowdy and boisterous. Trivia night can be brutal."

"Boisterous," repeated Jonah, pulling out his phone. "I like that word."

"You're collecting words?" asked Anna, grinning as she wrapped an arm around my waist.

I pulled her tighter against me.

"Yeah. When I hear a word I like, I add it to my phone notes so I can use it later in my manuscript."

"You're manuscript?" I chuckled. "My, aren't we getting with the author lingo."

"Fuck off, Reed. You'll be laughing it up when my book is a total hit."

"You mean bestseller," added Hale. "They're called bestsellers. Songs are called hits."

"Shut up, asshats. Anna, wrap this shindig up so we can go."

I pulled her to face me and cupped her cheeks. "Happy?"

"Utterly blissful."

"Blissful. Hmm. Might want to give that one to Jonah for his manuscript."

She laughed and tipped up onto her toes. I met her halfway and kissed her mouth sweetly then stepped back, squeezing her waist.

"My students told me they've got even more friends who want to sign up for classes after seeing the routine."

"The ones from summer camp that Emma posted to your social media pages?"

"Yep. Emma is a lifesaver with promotion." Her brow lifted with excitement. "I think this is really going to work."

"I know it is, baby." I pressed another kiss to her forehead. "Everything is going to be amazing because you're amazing."

She took my hand and shook her head, cheeks turning pink. She walked me toward her parents to say goodbye. "You're going to spoil me, Reed. I'll expect you to say things like that the rest of my life."

The rest of her life? My heart hammered faster. Yes, indeed, we were on the same page.

I laced our fingers and gave her hand a squeeze, tugging her closer as we walked. "I'll be telling you how amazing you are when we're old and gray and rocking in our chairs on the porch."

"Promise?" She shot me that shy look she often gave me when she wasn't as confident as she seemed.

"Cross my heart, Anna. Always."

Bonus Scene

❦

When Anna First Met Reed

~ANNA~

Bouncing was my favorite. Daddy didn't let my big brothers bounce on the trampoline with me because they were too rough, he said. And Daddy was right. But they were boys, so I guess they couldn't help it.

Still, I loved my alone time. Just me and Sandy, jumping as high as we could. I held her out in front of me, giggling as the skirt of her pink dress billowed out with each bounce, just like my favorite blue tutu which I was wearing over my purple zebra leotard. Her blond hair flew up too, like mine.

I liked to pretend Sandy was my twin, except her eyes

were blue and mine were brown. She was the only girl in the house to talk to besides Mom, so we spent most of our time together.

"You wanna go higher?" I asked her.

Using my legs like my gymnastics teacher told me, I pressed my weight harder into the trampoline, hopping in a circle along the edge. A piece of Sandy's hair flopped in front of her eyes, so I reached up to move it on the next bounce. I didn't know my foot was so close to the spring when it slipped into the gap.

I screamed and fell sideways, reaching out with my hands and Sandy flying from my arms. When I hit the ground on my side and elbow, I couldn't help but cry, even though my brother Jonah said only sissies cried.

"Hey, there. Are you okay?"

Still laying on my side, biting my lip as silent tears leaked down my cheeks, I looked up just as a tall boy I didn't know squatted down and helped me sit up.

"Did you hurt yourself?" he asked gently.

I sniffled and shook my head, peeking at him with my head down because I was embarrassed.

"I'm not a sissy."

The tall boy smiled. "You're right about that. I don't know many sissies who could take a fall like that and not scream and complain about it."

It was getting close to Halloween and the weather had turned cooler, which made me wonder why I suddenly felt warm all over. Especially in my sleeveless leotard and tutu.

"Are you okay?" he asked again, brushing off some dirt from my elbow.

"Uh-huh. But I need to check Sandy." I pointed over his shoulder where my doll had fallen next to my brother Justin's dirt bike.

The boy turned and reached out a long arm, plucking Sandy up and handing her over. I straightened her dress, and he picked a leaf out of her hair. He was so gentle and thoughtful. Not like my brothers at all.

"I think she looks okay," he added, wiping a tear off my cheek with his thumb.

I couldn't help but stare at him even though my mom said it was rude to stare. His eyes were as blue as my tutu.

Before I knew what I was saying, I blurted, "I didn't know boys could be pretty."

Suddenly, his cheeks and ears turned pink, and he sort of laughed. It was a rusty sound that was sweet to my ears.

"Hey, Reed! Come on, man!" my brother Jonah yelled from the gate with a skateboard under his arm, his voice breaking all weird. Mom said it was because of the puberty. Whatever that was. "What are you doing?"

The tall boy, who must be Reed, laughed and helped me stand up. I kept Sandy tucked safely in one arm.

"Your little sister fell off the trampoline," he called back.

Jonah made a face and rolled his eyes. "So what. She's fine. Let's go, bro!"

He tore off down the driveway with his skateboard. Before the tall boy could get away, I held out my hand for a shake like Daddy did when he bumped into his friends at Victor's Diner.

"My name is Anna."

He laughed when he took my hand which made him even prettier. "I'm Reed."

"Nice to meet you."

"You too, Anna." He let go of my hand and tapped me on the nose with one finger before jogging after my brother down the driveway.

I snuggled Sandy closer, letting her watch him with me. "Did you see him, Sandy?" She didn't answer, but she never did. She kept all my best secrets, too, so I decided to tell her my newest one. "That's the boy I'm going to marry someday."

Thank you for reading!

If you enjoyed this novella, you might like my other small town romance titles:

Bright Like Wildfire

Parks and Provocation

Peaches and Dreams

If you enjoy sexy, funny contemporary, you might also enjoy my paranormal romcom series STAY A SPELL.

Printed in the USA
CPSIA information can be obtained
at www.ICGtesting.com
LVHW032204190923
758757LV00036B/966

9 781088 203521